Items should be returned on or befo
shown below. Items not already req
borrowers may be renewed in perso
telephone. To renew, please quote t.. ..umber on the
barcode label. To renew online a PIN is required.
This can be requested at your local library.
Renew online @ **www.dublincitypubliclibraries.ie**
Fines charged for overdue items will include postage
incurred in recovery. Damage to or loss of items will
be charged to the borrower.

Leabharlanna Poiblí Chathair Bhaile Átha Cliath
Dublin City Public Libraries

Leabharlann Sráid Chaoimhín

Kevin Street Library

Tel: 01 222 8488

Baile Átha Cliath
Dublin City

Date Due	Date Due	Date Due

JUDI CURTIN was born in London, then moved to Cork where she lived for many years. She trained as a teacher, but now she mostly just writes, and thinks about writing. She has written the Alice & Megan series of books for young readers: *Alice Next Door*, *Alice Again*, *Don't Ask Alice* and *Alice in the Middle*. She has also written three adult novels: *Sorry, Walter!*, *From Claire to Here* and *Almost Perfect*. She now lives in Limerick, with her husband, three children and two cats. (Tip for aspiring writers – *get a cat.*)

ROISIN MEANEY was born in Listowel, County Kerry and now lives in Limerick city. She divides her time between teaching in the Limerick School Project and writing books. Her first book in the Journals series, *Don't Even Think About It*, was published in September 2006. She's also had three adult novels published: *The Daisy Picker*, *Putting out the Stars* and *The Last Week of May*. She likes reading and eating chocolate, and occasionally talking to her two cats.

See if I care

JUDI CURTIN & ROISIN MEANEY

THE O'BRIEN PRESS
DUBLIN

First published 2007 by The O'Brien Press Ltd,
12 Terenure Road East, Rathgar, Dublin 6, Ireland.
Tel: +353 1 4923333; Fax: +353 1 4922777
E-mail: books@obrien.ie
Website: www.obrien.ie

ISBN: 978-1-84717-021-7

British Library Cataloguing-in-Publication Data
Curtin, Judi
See if I care. - (Journals series)
1.Pen pals - Fiction 2.Young adult fiction
I. Title II. Meaney, Roisin
823.9'14[J]

1 2 3 4 5 6 7 8 9 10
07 08 09 10 11 12

The O'Brien Press
receives assistance from

Printed and bound in the the UK by J.H. Haynes & Co Ltd, Sparkford

To penfriends everywhere.

Acknowledgements

Thanks to Mary, Helen and all at
The O'Brien Press for their help, and to
all who had a hand, act or part in the
making of this book. Thanks to anyone
who pays good money for it, and thanks
especially to everyone who curls up
someplace quiet to read it – we need
people like you.

LUKE

Just as he was going up to his room to write the first letter, Luke Mitchell gave himself a black eye.

It happened about halfway up the stairs, when his foot caught in a raggy bit of the carpet and he put up his hands to keep himself from falling – somehow he managed to whack himself in one eye with a corner of the notebook he was carrying.

'What happened to you?' His mother opened the front door as he came stumbling down, holding his hands over his eye.

'I fell up the stairs.' That sounded funny and made him giggle a bit, but his eye still stung. 'Ow.'

His mother shrugged her coat off and pulled Luke's hands away as she examined his eye. 'You'll live, but you'll have a fine shiner there tomorrow. Splash some cold water on it.'

'I fell up the stairs,' Luke told his father, but it was a bad day, and his father didn't turn his face from the wall.

The cold water helped a little. When the stinging had almost stopped, Luke trudged back upstairs to tackle his penfriend letter. It was the first letter he'd ever written in his life, apart from the ones he'd sent to Santa when he was small, and they didn't really count, according to his teacher.

Mrs Hutchinson said letter writing was becoming a lost art. 'Put up your hand if you've never written a letter, apart from Santa ones,' she said, and hands went up all over the class.

'When I was your age,' Mrs Hutchinson told them, 'everyone wrote letters. There was no email, or text, and certainly no mobile phones. We wrote to our friends and posted the letters, and I remember how excited I'd get when I saw an envelope with my name on it coming in through the letter-box.'

Mrs Hutchinson was somewhere between twenty-five and sixty. Luke wasn't very good at guessing people's ages. Her hair was bright red, but that could have been fake – maybe it was snow white underneath. And when she pressed her mouth together, a row of lines appeared above her top lip, like the folds of an accordion. She was probably quite old, at least thirty.

'Why do we need to write letters now, when we have all the other stuff that you said?' Luke asked her.

Mrs Hutchinson sighed and pushed her glasses higher up on her nose.

'Because writing letters is an exercise in patience,' she said. 'Because people nowadays have forgotten what it feels like to have to wait for something. And because maybe, just maybe, it'll help your spelling and grammar too. Oh, and no typing – I want you to practise your handwriting, so stay away from those computers.'

She had a friend, she told them, who was a teacher in England. 'In a school in Manchester, and they're all dying for Irish penfriends.'

Yeah, right, Luke thought, *just as much as we're all dying for English ones.*

'Can we choose a boy or a girl?' one of the girls asked, and everyone groaned when Mrs Hutchinson shook her head.

'They're going to pull your envelopes out of a hat. There are more girls than boys in that class, so it's the only fair way to do it. You take whoever you get.'

She handed out empty envelopes and got them to copy the address of the English school from the blackboard. 'Bring them back with a stamp on, and your letter inside, before Friday.'

'Will you be reading the letters?' a boy asked.

Mrs Hutchinson considered. 'Not unless you want me to – letters should be private. Just make sure they're interesting and polite, and watch your spelling. Use a dictionary to spell words you're not sure of.'

Now, as he wondered what on earth to write, Luke chewed the end of his biro and hoped like mad that a boy pulled his envelope out. It was bad enough having to write to anyone, but if he got a girl, it would be an utter disaster.

What did girls talk about? He had no idea, even with two sisters in the house. Anne was still such a baby, and Helen hadn't said a word to him in well over a year, unless you counted 'Pass the salt', or 'Shut up, you'.

He picked up the stamp he'd bought on the way home. It had a picture of a man's head on it. The man had long curly hair and looked like a right dork. Luke read *Patrick Sarsfield 1650 – 1693* underneath the picture. He licked the back of the stamp and stuck it upside down in the corner of his envelope.

'It's good to stand on your head,' he told Patrick

Sarsfield. 'It sends blood to your brain.'

Then he turned to the first page of the notebook he'd bought on his way home from school. What on earth could he say?

Not the truth anyway – no way could he write the truth. Nobody would want to hear that. After a few minutes he took the biro out from between his teeth and began.

Dear Penfriend,

My name is Luke Mitchell. I'm eleven years and eight months old, and one hundred and fifty-three centimetres tall, and I have jet black hair with electric blue tips, and my nose and left eyebrow are pierced. I have a tattoo of a unicorn on my shoulder, and I'm a genius on the computer.

My older sister is a model and is often on the cover of magazines. My father is an astronaut and is training to be the first Irishman in space. We live in a big house out the country, with a lake in the back garden, and we own three racehorses. Their names are Thunder, Rocket and Diamond. Last year Rocket won a race in Leopardstown, which is a big famous racecourse in

Dublin, and we got €10,000. My father bought me a new laptop computer, the latest model.

In my spare time I like mountain climbing and white water rafting. I've climbed Carrauntouhill, Ireland's highest mountain, three times, and last summer I went white water rafting in Turkey. What are your hobbies?

Must go now – I have tons of homework.

Yours sincerely,
Luke Mitchell

ELMA

Elma stamped her way down the school corridor and out the front door, closing it behind her with a huge ear-shattering slam. Boys, boys, boys! Everywhere she went that day, there were boys causing her trouble. When she'd got up that morning, her two brothers, Zac and Dylan, were sitting on the landing, with their usual list of questions: were there any clean trousers, where were their schoolbags, and what was for breakfast?

When Elma got downstairs, things weren't much better. Out in the back yard, Snowball, the huge boy-Alsatian (and the ugliest creature in the history of the world) was howling for his food. And when she brought out his bowl, piled high with stinky brown jelly stuff, Snowball didn't even lick her hand in gratitude like dogs are supposed to. Instead he bared his huge yellow teeth, and looked at her as if to say – *be quicker next time, or I just might bite your hand off.*

When Elma finally got to school, Evil Josh, the meanest boy in the world, spent the whole day calling her names and doing his best to get her into trouble. And then the worst thing of all happened ...

Mrs Lawrence had been going on for weeks about her friend, Mrs Hutchinson, who was a teacher in Ireland, and how the children in her year wanted to be penfriends with the children in Mrs Lawrence's year. That was bad enough, but then it turned out that there were more girls in Elma's year, and more boys in Mrs Hutchinson's year, and so they would have to draw names from a hat, so that it would be fair. And of course, Elma picked a boy's name, someone called Luke. Darren, who sat next to her, picked a girl's name, and Elma wanted to swap, but swotty Darren said he wanted to abide by Mrs Lawrence's decision, and besides, he didn't have any problem about corresponding with a girl. And then Elma ended up in trouble, and she hadn't kicked Darren that hard at all, really.

So now she had to be penfriends with this stupid Luke Mitchell. And when Mrs Lawrence handed out the letters, Tara and Emily and all the other girls at her table got great girly letters, all decorated with hearts and flowers and stuff, and Elma got a big heap of ugly writing and lies from Luke Mitchell. As if that wasn't bad enough, Luke seemed to be too stupid to stick on his stamp properly, so Elma was the only one in the whole class who got an envelope with an upside-down stamp.

Tara was nice, though. When it was her turn for the computer that afternoon, she spent ages on the Internet, and she found out for definite sure that Luke Mitchell seemed to have mixed up truth and fiction. There was no space programme in Ireland, so his dad couldn't be an astronaut. She also discovered that even though Leopardstown really is a racecourse (and not a zoo like it sounded) no horse called Rocket had ever won a race there – ever. So that was another big fat lie.

Still, Elma wasn't exactly planning on telling the whole truth either, whenever she got around to answering Luke the Liar's letter. But she was just going to tell small lies; ones that stupid Luke would never know were lies; ones that didn't matter at all, really. After all, the full truth of Elma's life was much too sad to expose to a rich and happy Irish boy who climbed mountains for fun.

When she got to the school gate at the end of the day, Zac and Dylan were there – waiting, as usual – waiting for Elma to take charge of their lives.

As soon as they got home, the boys followed her around the house asking lots of questions. Some were easy, like, 'what's seven plus six?' or 'how do you spell monkey?' but some were harder, like, 'can I have two pounds for school?' and 'what's for tea?'

Dad was lying on the couch watching the National Geographic Channel on TV, and acting like he didn't have three children. This wasn't unusual, though, that's what he did all day every day. Elma felt like running in and shaking him and demanding that he help her. She didn't bother, though. She'd given up on him ages ago. She knew exactly what he'd say. *Sorry, Princess. I'd love to help you but I can't. My back's very bad today. If you're going through the kitchen, though, throw on a few fish fingers for me.*

So, as usual, Elma had to tidy up the breakfast things that were still scattered around the kitchen, and make the tea. And as usual, Snowball was outside pacing the yard, and growling every now and then, just because that was the kind of thing he seemed to do for fun.

It was late by the time Elma got upstairs to start her homework. She heard her mother's key in the front door, but ignored it. She was too tired for a chat; too tired to pretend that she'd had a nice day. She closed the door of the bedroom she shared with the boys. (The house only had two bedrooms, and her parents needed one to fight in.) She pushed Zac's comics off the small table in the corner, ripped a page from an old exercise book she found on the bed, scrabbled around on the floor until she found a pen that worked, and started to write.

Dear Luke Mitchell,

Thanks for your letter. My name is Elma Davey. I'm eleven years old, and too grown up to add on the months of my age like some people do. I haven't got any tattoos.

I live in a lovely house near Manchester, with my mum, my dad, and my sweet little sister, Jessica. Jessica is only ten months old, but she can say lots of words already. She has long blonde hair, and she loves it when I brush it for her.

Lucky you, having three racehorses. Next time why don't you send me a picture of you standing next to them? I'd love to see that.

We were going to buy a racehorse once, but it turned out that my mum was allergic, so we got a kitten called Snowball instead.

She's all grown up now. (Snowball, I mean, not my mum. Mum was grown up already.) She sleeps on my bed, because I'm her favourite person in the whole world.

My hobbies are ballet, and playing the violin and playing with Snowball.

Must go – this is my homework, and I think it's finished.

Yours sincerely,
Elma Davey

LUKE

When he was eight, Luke ate his two front teeth. It happened on the day that everything changed.

He was playing a tin whistle at the time – or rather, playing *with* it, since he didn't know how to play it. It was stuck in his mouth and his fingers were hopping over the holes and he was blowing into the mouthpiece, loudly. He was sitting in the back of the car, on the way home from a birthday party. The tin whistle had been in his party bag.

Luke remembered his dad saying, 'Would you ever give that–' and then Luke's head was flung forward, and the tin whistle banged into the front passenger seat, and rammed back against Luke's teeth with such force that it knocked the two front ones right out of his gum. Luke felt them in his mouth for a second, just before he swallowed them.

Then lots of things happened very quickly. The door beside Luke was thrown open, and he was pulled out and almost smothered in someone's coat. A woman started dabbing at his face with her hanky, and told him he'd be fine, he was a great boy.

And Luke could feel the wetness in his mouth, something gushing from someplace and filling it up, so he had to keep spitting, which Mum had always told him was one of the rudest things you could do, but nobody seemed to mind.

His mouth was sore, and the spit was red, which scared him.

He tried to ask people where his dad was, but he couldn't get the words out properly. He pulled his head out of the woman's hands and looked back towards the car, but there were too many people standing around it.

He couldn't see his dad. Something was thumping in his head.

Then he was sitting in the back of someone else's car that smelt like leather, and a woman – not the one with the hanky – was sitting beside him with an arm around his shoulders, saying 'We're taking you to the hospital, you'll be fine.' And because there was nothing else he could do, Luke leant against her black jacket and held the bundle of tissues she gave him to his mouth, and stopped trying to ask her if his dad was OK.

In the hospital he was lifted up onto a trolley, and a coffee-skinned woman in a white coat looked into his mouth and told him that he'd have to ask Santa to get him back his two front teeth for Christmas. Then she gave him a blue drink to rinse out his mouth, and a silver coloured bowl to spit into.

Finally, after lots of rinsing, Luke wiped his mouth with a paper towel and managed to say, 'Where's my dad?' His tongue felt too big, and the words sounded muffly.

The woman didn't look up from the clipboard she was writing on. 'I don't know, lovey, but I'll find out for you. We're looking for your teeth in the car, by the way – we might be able to stick them back in if we can find them quickly.'

'I think I swallowed them,' Luke told her, and she looked up.

'You did?'

'I think so.' He wondered if they'd have to cut a hole in him somewhere to fish out his teeth, but the woman just nodded.

'It doesn't matter – they won't do you any harm,

and you can get false ones. Now, where can we get in touch with your mum?'

After Luke told her the name of the travel agency where his mother worked, she went away, and he was left sitting on the trolley in the corridor. His mouth throbbed as he listened to the crying and shouting all around him. He watched the doctors and nurses rushing past with tight faces.

He wondered where his party bag was. He remembered there was a little green dinosaur in it, and a mini Crunchie bar. He loved Crunchies.

It seemed like an awfully long time before his mother came hurrying through the glass sliding doors, although he found out later that it was only about twenty minutes.

Her eyes searched the groups of people till she found him. 'God, are you alright?' She still wore her red work blazer, and her hands shook as she put them on his shoulders. 'Where are you hurt?'

'I swallowed my teeth,' Luke told her, and she drew her breath in sharply.

'Show.'

He lifted his top lip and she peered closely at his top gum. 'Is it sore?'

'Not very,' he lied, because she looked so scared.

'Were you wearing a seat belt?'

Luke thought for a second about lying again, but then he shook his head. 'I forgot. I had a tin whistle from my party bag, and it banged against my teeth and they fell out.'

She pressed her mouth closed and rubbed his arm.

Then, because Luke had to know, he said, 'Where's Dad?'

His mother closed her eyes, and Luke looked at the blue veins in her eyelids. Suddenly he didn't want her to answer.

'He's still unconscious. We'll have to wait till later to find out.' She put out her two hands. 'Come on, I'd better get you home. Careful now.'

Luke hopped down easily from the trolley. He looked up at his mother. 'I don't want to go home without Dad.'

But already she was walking him towards the door. 'I'll come back later – it could be ages, and I have to collect Anne from the Farrell's.'

Luke's father didn't come home for four months. Helen was the only one of the children old enough to visit him, and she came back from the hospital pale and silent, and slammed her bedroom door to keep Luke and his questions out.

His mother never mentioned Luke's father either –

not unless Luke asked her, and then she just said, 'Getting better'. Granny came to stay with them for a while, and moved into four-year-old Anne's room.

When their father finally came home, Anne wouldn't go near him. She hid behind Granny's dress, sucking her thumb and watching him as he shuffled slowly around, pushing his walker in front of him.

He looked at Luke as if he hardly knew him. 'Well,' he said, in a voice that didn't sound familiar. 'How are you getting on?'

'Fine,' said Luke, but his father had turned his head sharply towards the window, and was staring out. His hair was too long, and he was thin, and he had a black and grey beard.

'Look,' his father said, in a soft voice. 'Look, the ... ' He frowned, trying to think of the word. His thin finger pointed shakily at a small, brown chirping bird on the hedge. 'Look, there.'

And Luke looked out the window, and he knew that everything had changed.

His father never went back to work at the bank. A few of the people he'd worked with came to see him, soon after he came home, and sat with him in the living room, sipping tea loudly and talking about the weather, and how lucky Luke's father was not to have to head out in it.

When Luke was sent in by his mother to see if they wanted more tea, they kept him talking for ages, asking him about school, and wanting to know what soccer team he followed.

His father played with a loose button on his jacket sleeve, and didn't join in the talking. He slept in the dining room now, not upstairs any more.

As they were leaving, one of the people from the bank gave Luke's mother an envelope that she pushed quickly into her pocket.

And now, nearly three years later, Luke's mother still wasn't talking to Luke's father. She looked after him, because she was his wife, and because he couldn't. She fed him and she helped him to bed, she cut his nails and his hair, she shaved off his beard and she washed him, but she never talked to him.

He'd drunk two glasses of wine at the birthday party, when he went to pick up Luke. In the car he hadn't told Luke to put on his seat belt. And a quarter of an hour later he'd driven through a red light, straight into the path of a jeep.

Two days after he came home from hospital, Anne started wetting the bed. It still happened at least three times a week, even though she was seven now.

As soon as Mam left for her overtime, after tea

every Tuesday and Thursday, Helen went out with her friends instead of doing her homework. And Granny, who never went back to live in her own house, and who was supposed to be in charge when their mother was out, said nothing, because she didn't want to make things any worse than they were.

Luke looked at the letter in front of him, written on a ragged-edged copy page – at least *he'd* used a proper notebook for his letter. He wondered if this Elma had asked him for a photo of the horses because she suspected he was lying about them.

Not that he cared. It was only a stupid penfriend, not anyone he was ever going to meet. And even if he did meet her, he still wouldn't care.

Trust him to get a girl, who sounded like a right dork, with a cat called Snowball, and her dorky sister – and how could someone only ten months old have long hair? Luke thought babies that age would still be practically bald. So this Elma was probably lying to him too, which would be the only interesting thing about her.

And what did she mean, she was too grown up to add on the months of her age, 'like some people'? Was she getting at him? What was wrong with being exact about how old you were? Stupid girl.

His stamp this time had a picture of a man with a little moustache and round glasses. Under his head Luke read *James Joyce 1882 – 1941*. James Joyce looked a lot more interesting standing on his head.

Luke sighed and pulled his notebook towards him. Better get it over with.

Dear Penfriend,

Adding on the months of my age only goes to show that I like being accurate – it has nothing to do with how grown up I am, OK? Being accurate is very important if you're a top brain surgeon, which is what I'm planning to be. Imagine if you drilled a hole in someone's head three millimetres to the left of the spot you were supposed to drill. You wouldn't last very long (and neither would your patient, ha ha).

I'm wondering how come a ten-month-old baby could have long blonde hair, like you say your sister has. I didn't think hair grew that quickly on babies. It just sounds a bit funny to me, that's all.

Sorry I can't send you a photo of the horses – the only ones we have are framed, and hanging on the wall in the sitting room. When Rocket won his race last year we took a load of photos, of course, but unfortunately the house was robbed soon after the race, and all the photos were stolen. I'll tell the horses you said hello, though.

If you don't mind my saying so, I think Snowball is a bit of a dorky name for a cat. If I had a white cat (I'm guessing yours is white) I'd probably call it something like Popcorn or Milky Bar Kid. Or I might go for something totally different, like Midnight or Coal.

So you play the violin. I once thought about learning to play the tin whistle, but then I didn't bother.

Anyway, not much news from here. Our mid-term break is coming up in a couple of weeks, and my dad and I are taking a trip to Spain, to climb in the Pyrenees.

Gotta go,

Luke

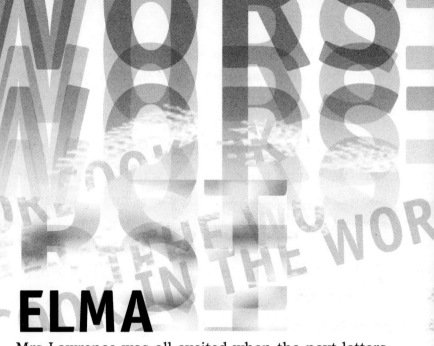

ELMA

Mrs Lawrence was all excited when the next letters arrived – like letters from stupid, lying penfriends were such a big deal. She handed them out with a big ceremony, as though she was handing out maps to a treasure island or vouchers for trips to Disneyland or something.

'Here's your letter, Tara, and what nice neat writing your penfriend has.'

'And yours, Ellen. Look, your friend has decorated the whole envelope with tiny flowers.'

'Hmm, Elma Davey, looks like your penfriend doesn't know up from down. Look at the stamp. Poor James Joyce is standing on his head.'

Elma took her letter, and said nothing. OK, so

Luke Mitchell was a big stupid boy, but she didn't want the teacher and the whole class mocking him. That was her job.

She opened the letter and read it quickly. Then she read it again, a bit more slowly. She smiled to herself. Maybe Luke Mitchell wasn't as stupid as she'd first thought. Still, if he was going to be a brain surgeon, he'd better learn how to tell the truth. She could just imagine him – *Mr Smith, now I know why you're getting headaches: you've actually got three brains, and one of them appears to belong to an anteater.*

Still, that was a clever answer about the racehorses. She knew that Luke had made them up, though, and she wasn't letting him away that lightly.

And he was right about the non-existent baby's long hair. What could she have been thinking of? No baby would have long blonde hair. Still, she couldn't change what she'd written.

Elma laughed out loud when she got to the bit about Snowball. Luke thought he was so clever, mocking her pet's name. Whatever would he think if he knew Snowball was a huge fierce Alsatian with a growl that could frighten children two streets away, and breath that could make an oak tree wilt?

Suddenly Elma felt a bit sad. Christening

Snowball was one of the last things Dad had done, back when he had a sense of humour. That was before the accident. Back when everything was different.

It was another horrid day. Evil Josh spent the whole afternoon whispering in her ear and calling her his favourite mean name – Lumpy Gravy Davey. It wasn't fair. After all, it wasn't her fault that the gravy on school dinners was always lumpy. OK, so Elma's mother was the dinner lady, but that was hardly Elma's fault, was it? Elma was sure that having your mother as dinner lady in your school must be the worst thing ever. It was bad enough when all she had to do was heat up the Turkey Twizzlers. Now, though, when dinner ladies were expected to cook 'real food', it made things doubly bad for Elma, because her mother was probably the worst cook in the world.

First there was the teasing she got from the other children (and with Evil Josh around, there was always plenty of that). The second bad thing was that her mother always gave her huge portions of everything, so she had to eat more lumpy gravy than anyone else. It was cruelty to children, and there should be a law about that kind of thing.

Dad was still in bed when she got home, so once

again Elma had to tidy the house and cook the tea. It was after half past seven when Mum got in. She threw herself into a chair, and said, 'I'm so tired, and my feet are killing me. Make me cup of tea, Elma, there's a love.'

Elma felt like saying that she was tired too, and that her feet were killing her after doing all the housework and taking Snowball on his walk, and that she still hadn't started her homework. But she didn't say any of that. Complaining never changed anything.

Even since Dad's accident, Mum had been doing three jobs. She left the house early in the morning to do her first cleaning job. Then she did the dinner-lady thing, and after that she had another cleaning job. Sometimes Elma thought that having all those jobs wasn't just about the money. Sometimes she thought Mum worked so much because she couldn't bear to be around Dad during the day. But how could Elma say that? It would only lead to another big fight, and in the end nothing would change – it never did.

So Elma made her mother a cup of tea, and then made her way upstairs to start her homework.

Zac was already asleep in bed. He looked cute, sucking his thumb and cuddling his teddy. She would have liked to write to Luke about him, but it was a bit late for that. How could she suddenly invent a six-year-old brother? As far as Luke was concerned, her only sibling was the unusually long-haired Jessica.

Dear Luke Mitchell,

Thank you for your letter. It was very interesting. I don't think I'd like to be a brain surgeon – sounds a bit messy to me – all that blood and gooey stuff. How would you eat your dinner after that? When I grow up I think I'll just be a pop star or something.

Don't Irish babies have long hair? What about your famous model sister? Was she a bald baby? Trust me, Jessica's hair is really beautiful. This morning I put it in two plaits, and tied them up with pink ribbons. She looked soooo sweet.

That's very sad about all your pictures of Rocket being stolen. He must have been in the newspaper, though, after winning such a big prize. Why don't you send me the date so I can look it up on the Internet?

Anyway, Mrs Lawrence (my teacher) said we have to tell our penfriends more about our lives, so here goes.

My mum is a chef in a very famous restaurant. Every day hundreds of people eat the food she cooks. Some people eat there every single day of the week – they even have their own special tables. She's especially famous for her gravy – it's the talk of the town where I live.

Our mid-term isn't too far away either. I'm not sure what we are going to do. Jessica's a bit young for mountain climbing, so we might just go to Disneyland or somewhere like that. I'm a bit fed up of Disneyland (after all, I've been there six times), but it will be nice for Jessica.

Must go now and practise my violin.

Bye for now,
Elma

LUKE

Helen was missing.

The first Luke knew that something was wrong was on his way downstairs for breakfast. His mother was on the phone in the hall, her free hand pulling at her hair, and this is what Luke heard as he came down the stairs:

'Look, she's bloody sixteen years old, that's a child in my ... well, you *should* be. Look, for God's sake, she's been out all ... I *know*, you already *told* me that, but there's got to be *something* ... well that's just *not* good enough–'

She looked at Luke as he walked past her, but kept on talking angrily into the phone.

His grandmother and Anne were sitting at the

kitchen table. Granny turned quickly as the door opened, then sagged a bit as Luke walked in.

He closed the door behind him. 'What's going on?'

'Helen never came home last night.' Her face was twisted with worry. 'She wasn't home when I was going to bed, but I thought she'd be in any minute ... and your mother just assumed she was there when *she* got in ...'

There was a piece of unbuttered toast on her plate. It looked as if it had been there for a while.

'Her bed hasn't been slept in,' Anne told Luke, and then ate a spoonful of Weetabix.

'Wow.' Luke thought of his sister, out all night in the dark. He tried to think of something to say that might take the lines out of his grandmother's forehead. 'Maybe she went to a friend's house, and just forgot to say.'

'Maybe.' His grandmother nodded slowly, still frowning. 'She might have done that, I suppose.'

'Who's Mum on the phone to?'

Before his grandmother had a chance to answer, Luke's mother burst into the kitchen and crossed quickly to the worktop by the sink and leant up against it, folding her arms. 'They're useless, bloody useless.' Her shoulders were hunched.

'What did they say?' Luke's grandmother started to

stand up, and then changed her mind and sat down again.

'They can't do anything until she's been missing for twenty-four hours, can you believe it?' His mum unfolded her arms and began to pace quickly around the kitchen, biting at one of her nails.

Then she stopped suddenly and glared at Luke's granny. 'Why did you let her go out? She's barely sixteen, Mam – what were you thinking of?'

Granny bit her lip, shaking her head. 'I'm sorry, Breda, I–'

But Luke's mother wasn't listening. She turned to Luke. 'Do *you* know any of her friends?'

He shook his head. Helen had been a mystery to him for a long time now. Since their father had come home from hospital, Luke had felt Helen pulling herself away from the family, little by little. Coming home later from school, disappearing after tea on the nights Mam worked late, and at the weekends. Spending the rest of the time in her room.

Luke had no idea what kind of life his older sister was leading. She barely spoke to him, to any of them. 'She's probably in a friend's house,' he said to his mother, but she wasn't listening to him any more either. Her head was bent over the phone book.

Luke wondered if he and Anne would have to go to

school, with his sister missing. But when Mr Farrell's car horn sounded outside, a few minutes later, nobody said, 'Of course you can't possibly go to school today', so he took the two lunchboxes from the fridge and picked up his bag and walked out into the hall with Anne. He wished he'd had something for breakfast – now he'd have to wait till half twelve to eat the tomato sandwich that was always gone soggy by lunchtime.

The curtains were still pulled in their father's downstairs bedroom. Their father had taken sleeping tablets every night since the accident, and he never got up now till around noon. On bad days he was still in bed when the children got home from school.

'Don't tell about Helen,' Luke said to Anne as they walked towards Mr Farrell's car.

'Why not?'

'Because it's none of their business.' No need to give anyone another reason to talk about the poor Mitchells. 'She'll be back soon anyway.'

Every so often during the day, Luke remembered that Helen was missing. He wondered what the others in his class would say if he told them. Would it get into the newspapers? Would Helen's photo be on 'Crimecall'?

What if she was dead? He couldn't eat his lunch,

thinking about that. He watched a few of his friends playing soccer in a corner of the yard. He hoped Helen would be found quickly, if she was dead. He didn't like to think of her lying in a field somewhere, with rain falling on her.

In the afternoon, Mrs Hutchinson asked them how they were getting on with their penfriends. A few girls said 'brilliant', and Luke guessed that they were writing to boys. None of the boys in the class said brilliant.

'Well, they're delighted with you, according to their teacher,' Mrs Hutchinson told them. 'Keep up the good work.'

Helen came home that evening. She walked into the kitchen as her mother was giving a description of her to a policewoman.

From the sitting room, Luke cocked his head and listened to the shouting. As soon as he made out Helen's voice, he turned up the volume on the TV. His father, sitting in another armchair, kept his eyes on the screen, but began rocking uneasily as soon as the shouting began.

'Helen came home,' Luke told him. His father darted a look at him, and then stared back at the screen, still rocking.

'It's OK,' Luke said. 'She's home now. Everything's

OK.' When 'The Simpsons' was over, he watched the credits as they rolled up the screen. 'Will I switch to the News?'

'Yeah, the News,' said his father, brightening up. 'Yeah, the News.'

In the hall, Luke stood listening for a minute. There was no shouting coming from the kitchen. The police car was gone from the driveway. He could smell the sausages they always had on Wednesdays, and his mouth watered. He remembered he'd had nothing to eat all day.

Helen didn't come down for tea. Luke's grandmother put sausages and pudding and grilled tomato on a plate and brought it upstairs. His mother looked as if she'd been crying.

Afterwards, Luke helped with the dishes while his mother put his father to bed.

'Where was Helen?' he asked his grandmother, but she just shook her head.

'She won't say. She wouldn't even tell the guard.' She finished scrubbing the frying pan and put it on the draining board.

In his room later, Luke reread his penfriend's last letter. She still sounded so dumb. 'I think I'll be a pop star' indeed. As if you could just decide to be something like a pop star, and that would be it. As if a pop star was better than a brain surgeon. Not that Luke had any notion of being a brain surgeon, of course.

And how on earth was he going to get out of the whole horse business? Why hadn't he thought more about what stories to make up? His penfriend was being so persistent – it was obvious she didn't believe he had any horses. Well, no way was he going to admit that. He'd just have to think of something.

And what the heck was all that about her mother being a famous chef? How could anyone be famous for making gravy? Wasn't that just powder mixed with hot water? What a load of rubbish – famous for making gravy. At least his horse story sounded like it might be true.

He addressed the envelope and stuck the stamp on while he was thinking about what to write. The picture on the stamp was some kind of modern art painting that looked exactly the same upside down.

He lay on his bed and thought for a while. Then he sat up, pulled the notebook onto his lap and began.

Dear Penfriend,

It's been the worst week of my life. On Tuesday Rocket fell while he was in training and broke his leg, and had to be put down. The whole family is devastated. Rocket's trainer said he'd never have another horse like him. I'm too upset to even talk about the race now.

You asked about my sister having long hair as a baby. I'm wondering what on earth that would have to do with her being a model now. Anyway I haven't a clue what kind of hair she had when she was small – I just said that I didn't think babies had long hair. No biggie – get over it.

My dad and I had a brilliant mid-term break in the Pyrenees. We had two excellent climbs, and we stayed in a 5-star hotel with a Jacuzzi in the bathroom. I had octopus for dinner on the first night. It was a bit salty but OK. I like to try new food whenever I travel.

Speaking of food, I never heard of someone being famous for making gravy. You learn something new every day – although if I was famous for something I cooked, I'd rather it was something a bit more exciting than gravy.

Sorry, but I'm just not in the mood to write any more.

I keep thinking about Rocket.

Luke

PS I've never heard of a pop star who played the violin. Maybe you should just join a world famous orchestra instead.

ELMA

Elma smiled to herself as Mrs Lawrence handed her the letter. Once again the stamp was upside down, though it was a modern art stamp and she had to look carefully to be sure. This upside-down thing couldn't be an accident, could it? Surely no one could be that stupid? Maybe Luke Mitchell was trying to send her a secret message.

Of course Tara got yet another beautiful envelope – this time it was all covered in mauve and blue stars. Still, Elma thought to herself, Tara's penfriend sounded really boring, always going on about schoolwork and history projects and stuff, and at least that couldn't be said about Luke Mitchell. She could think of lots of bad things to say about him –

he was vain and boastful and a big fat liar, but at least he wasn't boring.

She wondered if there was any truth in the story about Rocket. She knew he'd never won at Leopardstown, but maybe he had existed. Maybe he really had died, and maybe Luke was really sad. If Snowball was a cat instead of a monster-dog, Elma would miss him if he died. Maybe it was time to stop going on about Rocket, just in case.

And maybe it was time to stop arguing about Jessica's hair, too. Since Jessica didn't actually exist, maybe it was best not to spend too long arguing about how long her hair was?

When Elma got home, she quickly forgot about Luke Mitchell and his strange letters with the upside-down stamp. The kitchen was filthy, just like she had left it in the rush for school that morning. Clearly, Dad had once again spent the whole day in bed, watching television.

Elma was really cross as she tried to tidy up. So cross that she kept banging doors and slamming things into cupboards. So cross that Dylan and Zac didn't argue once. So cross that they even tried to help her without being asked. Dylan vacuumed the living room, while Elma and Zac washed the breakfast stuff. It was really hard because all the food was dried up and stuck on to the dishes.

Zac chatted away about his teacher as he dried the glasses. Then he struggled to reach the cupboard to put them away. Elma wiped her hands.

'Wait a sec,' she said. 'I'll help you.'

Zac grinned at her. ''s OK, Elma. I'm big. I can do it.'

He scrambled on to the kitchen counter. Elma laughed as he did a little wriggle of victory. But then, as he reached for the first glass, disaster struck. He lost his balance and tumbled towards the floor.

Elma watched as if it were happening in slow motion. Zac's small, grubby hand grabbed for the counter, but missed, and knocked the glass to the floor, where it smashed into tiny pieces. A second later Zac fell on top of it with a dull thud. There was a moment's silence before the screaming started. Elma hauled Zac to his feet, and felt a sudden cold chill when she saw that there was a deep cut on his cheek. She grabbed the damp and rather smelly tea towel and held it to his face. Dylan came in to see what the screaming was about.

'Quick,' Elma said. 'Run up and wake Daddy, and tell him Zac has hurt his face.'

Seconds later Dylan was back. 'Daddy said to put a plaster on it, and to make him stop crying because Daddy has a sore head and needs his sleep.'

By now the bleeding had almost stopped, and Zac's crying had turned to small, quiet sobs. Elma felt like crying now.

How could her dad be so mean?

Didn't he even care that Zac was hurt? Didn't he care enough to drag himself out of bed to see how bad the cut was? Didn't he care about anything or anyone beside himself?

Elma sat Zac on the couch and dialled her mother's mobile. She'd been warned to do that only in an emergency, and surely this was an emergency?

A few hours later, Zac was home from hospital, with three painful-looking stitches in his cheek and a huge lollipop in his mouth. Elma's mother went upstairs, and minutes later the shouting started.

Elma could only hear bits of it, all in her mother's voice.

'... the poor child could have been scarred for life ...'

'... threatening us with social services ...'

'... he kept saying his big sister was minding him ...'

'... she's only eleven ...'

'... stupid layabout father ... '

'... no good to any of us ...'

Zac and Dylan were huddled on the couch, looking frightened. Elma closed the door and turned the television up loud. Poor Zac and Dylan couldn't really remember the time before the accident, when they were a normal happy family. Sometimes Elma had to struggle to remember it herself.

Back in those happy times, Dad went out to work as a plumber every day and Mum stayed home and minded the children. They were like a happy-ever-after family in a storybook. And then one day the happy-ever-after came to a sudden end.

A lorry arrived on the building site where her dad was working, and the back of the lorry opened unexpectedly, and three toilets fell out. Two of the toilets smashed to pieces on a patch of dried concrete. The third toilet knocked Dad to the ground, injuring his back. He spent three weeks in hospital, and hadn't been able to work ever since.

So, as well as having a sick dad, Elma also had to put up with the teasing at school. Why couldn't Dad have had a less embarrassing accident? She was now the girl whose dad couldn't work because a toilet fell on him. Harry's dad lost a leg in Iraq, and he was treated like a hero, and all Elma got was mockery. It just wasn't fair.

Dad's back got a bit better after a while, but it was like something had switched off in him. The doctor had told him his days as a plumber were over. He would never again be able to do a job that involved bending down to get at awkward pipes. But he could still work – if he wanted to. There were still lots of jobs he *could* do.

A man from the job centre dropped in a huge bundle of leaflets about retraining courses. They were still in a corner of the living room – unopened. (Sometimes Dylan And Zac used them for making paper planes.)

And now Dad didn't want to do anything except lie around in bed, or on the couch, watching TV. So that's what he did. All day. Every day. The National Geographic Channel had become the centre of his universe.

Life had been pretty bad ever since the accident. Elma didn't like school much, but it was better than being home with Dad. Mid-term had been awful. Really, really awful. Mum didn't have to do school dinners, but she did extra hours at her cleaning jobs. So Elma just hung around the house with the boys, and brought stuff upstairs, or into the living room for her dad, and counted the days to when she could go back to school and some kind of normality.

Both boys were asleep by the time Elma got around to writing her letter. Zac was snoring, and she could see a big bruise forming on his forehead. She'd have liked to tell Luke about what happened, but how could she? As far as Luke was concerned, Zac didn't even exist, so how could he have fallen down and cut himself badly? She wished she hadn't lied, but it was too late now.

She addressed her envelope first – the boring bit – best to get it over with. She wrote 'Luke' and then on a sudden whim, finished the 'e' with a curly line. It was meant to look kind of cool, but ended up looking a bit like a pig's tail. She hoped he wouldn't mind. When she'd finished writing the address, she grinned to herself as she peeled her stamp from its backing paper, and placed it firmly upside down on the envelope. She hoped the Queen wouldn't mind standing on her head. And she really, really hoped there wasn't a law against that kind of thing. Still, too late now, Mrs Lawrence had given her only one stamp, so it would have to do.

Would Luke notice?

If so, what would he think?

And why did she care what stupid liar Luke thought anyway?

Dear Luke,

I'm so sorry to hear about Rocket. I would be very sad if anything ever happened to Snowball. She's lying next to me now, purring. Her fur is all soft and warm.

Jessica got her hair cut last week. It's not so long now, but she's still cute.

I'm glad you enjoyed your mountain climbing. The only mountain I was on was Space Mountain in Disneyland Paris. It was soooo scary. I went on everything three times because my dad got special passes. Jessica's favourite ride was 'It's a Small World'.

Making gravy might not sound exciting, but believe me, it is. Mum's thinking of writing a book about it. She says gravy is the heart of every meal. I bet if you had tried some of my mum's gravy on your octopus it would have tasted much nicer.

Is it just you and your dad and your sister in your family? I didn't tell you about my dad yet, did I? He's great – really funny and exciting. He can't work at the moment. He had a terrible accident. A little girl wandered onto a building site and got trapped under a big heap of planks. She nearly died, but Dad heard her screams, and rescued her. The planks fell on him, and he hurt his back very badly. We hope he's going to be better soon, though.

Have to go now. Time for ballet class.

Your penfriend,

Elma

PS If you've never heard of a pop star playing violin, maybe you should get out more. Ever heard of Vanessa-Mae????????

There's NO way I'd ever play in an orchestra. It would be much too boring for me – more like the kind of thing for someone who wanted to be a brain surgeon.

LUKE

The horse butted his head impatiently against Luke's coat. This close, his body smelt like straw. He pushed his long nose up under Luke's armpit, snorting loudly.

'Hang on, hang on.' Luke pulled an apple out of his pocket and held it flat in his palm, just under the horse's nose. The horse sniffed it and then took it whole into his mouth and crunched it loudly. Little bits of apple flew out of his mouth.

Luke watched him, his hand wrapped around another apple in his pocket. He wondered what his mother would say if she knew that he saved his lunchbox apples so that he could feed them to a horse. He thought she'd probably go mad.

The horse wasn't sleek and graceful, like a racehorse. He was a big, heavy farm horse with a shaggy mane and enormous strong legs, and his name was Chestnut. He belonged to Luke's uncle Jack, who lived a few miles out of town, in the farmhouse he and Luke's father had grown up in.

Chestnut didn't work any more. For as long as Luke could remember, he'd spent his days in the field, pulling up the grass with his strong yellow teeth.

'What kind of work did he do?' Luke had asked Jack, when they were out visiting the farm one Sunday a few months ago.

'Everything the tractor does now. Ploughing, dragging, lifting – he was a strong old fellow in his time.'

Luke looked up at the huge horse. 'Did anyone ever ride him?' He imagined sitting way up there, his legs pressed against Chestnut's warm body, hanging on to the shaggy mane.

Jack nodded. 'Charlie did a bit, when she was younger.' Charlie was Jack's daughter, away at college now. 'But nobody's been up on his back for a long time.' He looked at Luke. 'Would you fancy it? He's very quiet – you'd be fine.'

Luke nodded, suddenly afraid to say anything.

'Right, tell you what – I'll collect you next Saturday,

on my way home from the market. That'll give me a chance to track down the saddle.' He paused. 'And if you stay around after and give me a hand with the cleaning-up in the yard, I'll give you a few euro for your trouble.'

And that was what happened, the next Saturday and most Saturdays since then. Jack called around to Luke's house after dropping Luke's aunt Maureen into the farmer's market, where she sold fruit cakes and apple tarts. The two of them drove out to the farm, where Luke spent his first hour riding Chestnut around the field, and the next two helping Jack to hose down and scrub out the yard, and change the straw in the stable where Chestnut lived, and feed the pigs, and do anything else that needed doing, before Jack drove him home again, on his way to collect Maureen.

Luke got fifteen euro from Jack every Saturday. When he tried to give it back the first time, feeling awkward, Jack said, 'If I got a stranger to help me, I'd pay him. Why wouldn't I pay you, just because you're family?' So Luke took it, and brought it home and hid it in an old custard tin at the back of his wardrobe.

And now, eighteen weeks later, he had two hundred and seventy euro saved. Still a long way to go for what he wanted.

On the way home, he asked Jack to drop him in town. 'I have things to get.'

'Fair enough.'

Luke walked down the main street, past the straggle of market stalls. He stopped outside Brady's Electrical and looked in the window, and there it was.

Snow white, shining, with two neat rows of buttons running along its top panel, and a round glass door like a stomach in the middle of it. The door was open, and a blue towel was hanging halfway out of the stomach. The folded piece of card sitting on the top still said €409 in black marker – one hundred and thirty-nine euro more than Luke had saved.

It was the washing machine he was going to buy for his mother, to replace the one that was worn out from washing Anne's wet sheets so often – or maybe just because it was so old, a wedding present from Granny and Grandpa Mitchell. It hadn't actually given up yet, but it clanked and rattled every time it was switched on, and Luke's mother lived in dread of it breaking down. Luke hoped he could save enough before that happened, but at the rate he was going, it would be well after Christmas, which was only six weeks away, by the time he had enough.

He turned to walk home, thinking hard. Was there anything else he could do to get more money? He passed a newsagent's, and paused. What about a paper round? How much did they pay?

He walked in. There was a tall, dark-haired man behind the counter, serving a teenage girl with lots of studs in her ears. Luke waited until the teenager walked out, and then he said, 'I was looking for a paper round.'

The man shook his head. 'Sorry, son – I have my regulars for that.'

'OK.' Luke turned to go. He should have known it wouldn't be that easy.

'Hang on–' The man rubbed his cheek. 'I could do with getting my car washed, if you're interested in making a few quid. No short cuts though – I'd expect a proper job.'

Luke stopped. He could wash a car; he'd often washed his mother's one. 'How much would you pay?'

The man considered. 'If you do a proper job, I'll give you a fiver.'

It didn't sound like brilliant pay to Luke. If the man had a big car, 'a proper job' could take quite a while. But it was worth a try. 'OK.'

It was a medium-sized Toyota, not too dirty-looking. It took Luke forty minutes to earn his five euro, and the man told him to call back once a week if he wanted.

When Luke got home, he sat in front of the ancient computer in a corner of his father's downstairs bedroom and typed:

Car Washing
A proper job guaranteed.
Reasonable price.
You won't be disappointed.

At the bottom he put his name and phone number, and then he printed it out. The printer creaked and groaned as the page appeared bit by bit.

'What's that?' asked his father from the armchair he spent most of the day in.

'My new job,' Luke told him. 'Car washing.'

'Car washing.' His father turned and looked out the window. The small blue hatchback Luke's mother had bought with the insurance money sat in the driveway. Luke wondered if his father remembered anything about the accident, or his life before it.

He thought again how strange that his penfriend's father should have been in an accident too. The difference was, it sounded like her father was going to get better.

Not like his, who would never be back to the way he was before. 'His brain was damaged,' their mother told the three children. 'That's why he can't remember things, and why it's a bit hard to talk to him the way we used to.'

'Is he still our dad?' Anne asked.

Helen snorted. 'Course he is, dummy.' But Luke knew what Anne meant.

He took the page about the car washing to his mother. 'Could you copy this at work for me?'

His mother read it and then looked at Luke. 'You want to wash cars?'

Luke shrugged. 'I thought I might try – you know, save a bit for Christmas.' He wondered if she remembered that Jack paid him every Saturday. He hadn't mentioned it for ages – not since he'd decided what to spend it on.

She thought for a minute. 'As long as you do your homework first.' She held up the leaflet. 'And you only do this around here, not all over the place.'

The next day she came home with twenty pages, and Luke went out before tea and shoved them through the letterboxes of the houses where he thought people might like someone to wash their cars: Mr Madden, and the Lehane's, and Mrs Lorrigan and Miss Looby, and the man at the end of the road who lived with his mother, whose name Luke didn't know, and a few on the next road who might be interested.

He wondered if anyone would phone him. Maybe everyone went to automatic car washes now – maybe nobody wanted a human car wash any more.

After tea, he decided to get his next penfriend letter done, even though it wasn't due until the middle of next week. He'd been feeling a bit guilty for telling her all those lies, especially as she seemed to believe that stupid story about Rocket breaking his leg and having to be put down, and the rubbish about him climbing mountains in Spain.

And even if she didn't believe him, at least she didn't say anything nasty.

He was sorry now for being so sarcastic about her mother's gravy, and about her violin playing – telling her to join a world famous orchestra – that was a bit mean. Mrs Hutchinson said people who used sarcasm were trying to be funny in a nasty way. She said sarcasm was 'the lowest form of wit'.

OK, no more lies. From now on, he'd tell her the truth. He picked up her envelope and looked at the way she'd written his name, with a little curled-up line, like a pig's tail, coming out of the end of the 'e'. Pity she had to be a girl, though.

Then, for the first time, he noticed the stamp. The Queen of England was standing on her head.

Luke stared. Was she copying him, or had she just stuck it on in a hurry without realising? Were English people allowed to stick the Queen on upside down?

He took Mrs Hutchinson's envelope from his schoolbag and wrote Elma's name and school address on it. Just for the laugh, he put a curled-up line coming out of the end of the 'y' of 'Davey'. She probably wouldn't even notice.

He stuck on some famous church, with its steeple pointing down, in the top right hand corner, and then he opened his notebook.

Dear Penfriend,

I'm sorry to hear about your dad. I hope he recovers soon. He sounds brave.

I have two sisters, one older and one younger. I'd like a brother, but I don't think I'll have one now.

It's funny you didn't think I had a mam. She works in a travel agency. My granny lives with us too – she moved in about three years ago – so there are six people altogether in my house. Sometimes it's a bit too many, especially when my older sister is in a mood.

No, I never heard of Vanessa-Mae. I don't listen to the radio much, I prefer my dad's collection of music. He has loads of stuff like The Beatles and The Kinks and The Doors and bands like that. My favourite band is Supertramp – have you ever heard of them? They were famous in the seventies, and they had loads of hits. One of their albums is called Breakfast in America (they're from there) and it's the name of a song too. They're cool.

Maybe I was wrong about your mother's gravy. It sounds like she knows a lot about it. I never knew there was more than one kind.

Well, that's about it,
Luke

PS I don't think I'd be much good in an orchestra, as the only thing I play is the fool (ha ha).

ELMA

As soon as the bell rang for break, Elma raced out of the classroom, across the playground and behind the bicycle shed. There she hid, clutching her side and panting as she struggled to catch her breath. She had to avoid Tara at all costs. Elma liked Tara very much. And Tara liked Elma. All the other girls in the class had given up on her years ago, soon after Dad's accident. But Tara was new in her school, and she still thought that Elma was a normal girl from a normal family. She thought that the only strange thing about Elma was her mother's bad cooking. Except for the lumpy gravy and the soggy carrots, she figured that everything was just fine with the Davey family. Tara knew about Dad's accident, of course, Evil Josh had seen to that, but she didn't know how bad things were at home. She had absolutely no idea.

Now though, everything was starting to go wrong. Tara was no longer satisfied with just being friends at school. She wanted to do other stuff with Elma, stuff that involved seeing each other outside school. And how could that ever happen?

Elma had to mind Zac and Dylan every day. If she left them with her dad, it just wouldn't be safe. It would be like leaving a baby in charge of her baby brothers. Since his accident, Elma hadn't trusted Dad very much, but after the day when Zac cut his face so badly, and Dad hadn't even managed to drag himself out of bed to see if it was serious, she knew he was no help at all. So there was no way Elma could leave the boys and go to Tara's house.

And how could she invite Tara to her house?

What if she saw the mess in the kitchen – the breakfast stuff all over the table, and probably some of the previous night's dinner things, too?

What if Tara looked out of the window, expecting to see a lovely garden with flowers and swings, and instead saw Snowball rampaging around the yard, snarling?

What if Tara saw Elma's dad, who hadn't shaved or

cut his hair in months, lying on a couch in his old tracksuit bottoms, and whining for a cup of tea and a ham sandwich?

What if Mum came home and there was a huge row?

No, it just wasn't even possible to think of it without feeling sick. She'd have to put Tara off.

But yesterday, Tara had been really pushy about it. 'We've been best friends for two and a half months now,' she said. 'It's time we did something fun. I'm going to ask my mum can we do something tomorrow. You can ask your mum, too. We could go to one of our houses for tea.'

Elma didn't know what to say. She'd already invented ballet classes on Monday and Wednesday afternoons, and violin lessons on Tuesdays and Fridays, and she'd said that she always did family stuff at the weekends. But she hadn't invented anything for Thursdays. And today was Thursday. But instead of just saying 'no', she'd said 'maybe', so now Tara was looking for her. And she was afraid if she put her off again, Tara would give up on her altogether, and she'd have no friend at all. There would be no one to defend her when Evil Josh called her names involving lumpy gravy and soggy carrots.

She peeped around the shed. She could see Josh

and his horrible friends strutting around like big ugly turkeys. She could see Tara looking all around the playground for her. She was glad when the bell rang. Back in the classroom, Tara came over. 'Where were you?' she asked. 'I was looking for you. What did your mum say about this afternoon?'

Elma half turned away. Even though she'd had plenty of practice, she still wasn't very good at telling lies (except in letters to Luke Mitchell, and that didn't really count.)

'Sorry, Tara,' she said over her shoulder. 'I was looking for you, too. I wanted to tell you I can't do stuff with you after school today. I forgot that I have to go to the dentist.'

Tara gave her a hug. 'You poor thing. Maybe next week.'

Elma put her head down. 'Yes,' she said, 'maybe.'

So instead of doing fun stuff in Tara's house, the afternoon was just like all the others. Walk the boys home. Clean the house. Cook the tea. Try to ignore Snowball growling, and the endless noise of yet another nature programme from the living room.

She was so busy that she forgot all about Luke's letter with the upside-down stamp, and the funny curly tail coming from the 'y' at the end of Davey.

As she sat down to do her homework, she pulled

the envelope out of her bag with one

She slipped the letter out and began to read.

When she was finished, she put the letter do

and thought for a while. Luke wasn't his usual self. Was it something she had said? He sounded kind of sad. Maybe it was because he had no brothers. Funny, really. He had no brothers, and she had no sisters. Maybe they should swap families or something. She made a face at the thought. Who'd want to swap families with her? Who'd volunteer to live her life? Not Luke Mitchell, with his perfect life, that was for sure.

He sounded like he really was sorry for what had happened to Dad. But that was only because he didn't know the truth. If he knew about the toilet, he'd just laugh. Like everyone else.

That was the good thing about Luke Mitchell. He only knew what Elma decided he should know. And if it was only half-true, or even not at all true, well ... he'd never know, would he? And what he didn't know couldn't hurt him. Could it?

She addressed her envelope with a curly 'e' in Luke, and a star with a face in it instead of a dot over the 'i' in Mitchell. She carefully stuck on her stamp upside down. Then she took a page and began to write.

...nny living with me. Both of mine died ...mind a brother either. If I had a brother, I'd ...Zac. Or maybe Dylan.

...a bit better these days. The parents of the girl he saved came visit last week, and that always cheers Dad up for a while.

I've heard about the Beatles, but aren't they all dead by now? I've never heard of Supertramp. Sounds like the big, tall old man who lives in a doorway near my school (ha ha). I like the sound of Breakfast in America. I had breakfast in Manchester this morning and it wasn't much fun.

Don't worry that you didn't understand about the gravy. Most people don't. Mum might just have part of the book about the gravy. The rest might be about vegetables. She's especially good with carrots. Do you like carrots?

Anyway, I've told you about my family, so now I'm going to tell you about my best friend. Her name is Tara. She just moved to our school this year. She used to live in London. She's really great fun. We sit next to each other at school.

We do loads of stuff after school, too. Most weekends we have sleepovers in each other's houses. This weekend it's her turn to come to my house. We always have lots of sweets, and sometimes we make popcorn. Mum and Dad let us stay up late to watch a DVD. Snowball loves Tara, and usually when she sleeps over we sneak her up to my bedroom and she sleeps on Tara's bed.

Must go,
Elma

PS One last question. Why do you stick your stamps on upside down?

LUKE

Nobody at all phoned him, the week after he dropped in the leaflets. Nobody seemed interested in getting a proper car wash from a real human.

The next Saturday he got his uncle Jack to drop him in town again, and he went into the newsagent's.

The same man was behind the counter. He looked up as Luke walked in. 'Hey there.'

'I've come to wash your car,' said Luke, wondering if he remembered him. 'I did it last week, and you said to come back.'

'I did indeed,' said the man. 'She's out the back, waiting for you.'

As the man was paying him afterwards, Luke got

an idea. 'Can I put a notice in your window about car washing?'

The man nodded. 'No problem. And I'll tell you what – if you're looking for business, my wife's car could do with a good wash. She's out at the moment, but she'll be here in about an hour, if you want to call back.'

That evening, Luke got three phone calls. Two of them were from people who'd seen his notice in the newsagent's window. The third was from Miss Lynch on the next street, who'd got his leaflet in her door the week before.

The next day, he got two more calls.

Over the next two weeks, he washed seven cars. He made thirty-five euro. With the thirty euro Jack gave him, he was only short seventy-four euro for the washing machine, and there was still nearly a month to go to Christmas.

He might just make it.

He spent most of his Sundays washing cars, but he didn't mind. It gave him a reason not to be at home.

Since the night she stayed out, Helen was forbidden to leave the house on school nights. Mam rang home three times on the evenings she was working late. When the phone rang, Helen waited for

Granny to answer it and call up to her, and then she stamped down the stairs and spoke in a sulky voice to Mam.

When Luke asked her if she'd ever heard of a pop star called Vanessa-Mae, Helen just ignored him. Nobody was allowed into her room. Sometimes when she passed Luke on the stairs, he smelt cigarettes. One morning he thought he heard her getting sick in the bathroom.

She never smiled. He couldn't remember what her smile looked like.

'Did you know there's more than one kind of gravy?' he asked Granny one evening.

She lifted her eyes from her book and thought. 'Well, I suppose you can make it with the meat juices, or just use gravy powder and water,' she said. 'But it wouldn't be very different really.'

'Would you buy a cookery book that just had gravy recipes in it?' Luke asked her.

She looked at him in amusement. 'I don't think so. What's brought all this on?'

Luke shrugged. 'Just something my penfriend said.'

His mother dropped two eggs on the kitchen floor one evening. They slipped out of her hands as she was taking them out of the fridge. She looked at the mess on the floor and then she burst into tears. She put her head in her hands and bent over the sink and cried and cried.

Luke put his hand on her shoulder. 'Please don't,' he told her. 'I'll clean them up, it's OK.' Her body shook with crying. They were the only two in the kitchen. 'Please, Mam,' he said. 'Please don't cry.'

He pulled two sheets off the roll of kitchen paper and gave them to her, and she dabbed her eyes and asked him what she'd do without him.

The eggs were slimy and hard to clean up. Mam took the mop from him. 'It's OK, I'll do it.' Her face was blotchy and all around her eyes was red and damp. 'Sorry, love – it's just been a long day.'

'Can't you phone work and tell them you're sick?' he asked. It was one of her overtime nights.

She shook her head. 'There's nobody there but me in the evenings – and anyway, we need the money. I'll be OK.' She'd started doing overtime after Luke's father had his accident – three extra hours in the evening twice a week – doing whatever could be done without the customers there.

'I'm saving up for a surprise for Mam,' Luke told his father. 'A big surprise.'

His father looked at his reflection in the window. He rubbed his chin and pushed his hair back from his forehead.

'Did you hear me?' Luke asked him. 'I'm getting a surprise for Mam.'

His father turned to look at him. 'Luke,' he said. 'Good boy.' Then he turned back to the window and watched Luke's mother getting into her car. His face didn't change as he looked at her.

Mrs Hutchinson suggested that they send Christmas cards to their penfriends. 'I know there's still a few weeks to go,' she said, 'but you won't be writing again till after Christmas. It would be nice for a change, instead of your usual letters.'

Luke looked through the cards in the newsagent's shop on the way home from school. The cheapest he could find cost three euro. He decided Elma would be just as happy with a letter.

He asked the woman in the post office if she had any special stamps for Christmas. She gave him one with a picture of a candle on it. It looked good upside down on the envelope, like a firework – or a rocket, just about to blast off.

Luke wrote Elma's name and school address. Then he turned the envelope around and drew a snowman on the flap. That was nearly as good as a card.

He looked out the window as he thought about what to write. Her last letter was pretty girly, with all that talk about sleepovers and stuff.

He really wished she was a boy – and although she lived in Manchester, he bet she didn't even follow Man United.

But for a girl, he supposed she wasn't too bad. He began to write.

Dear Penfriend,

Thanks for your last letter. I've got a new job washing cars. I charge five euro per car, and I've got lots of customers.

Two of the Beatles are still alive. They are Ringo Starr and Paul McCartney. Dad says Paul McCartney was the best Beatle, but I think I prefer John Lennon. He was shot by a mad guy in New York years ago – my dad remembers hearing it on the radio. And George Harrison died of some disease like cancer or something.

I never asked you if you support Man United. They've got a lot of fans over here, but I prefer Chelsea. They're from London, so maybe your friend supports them. Tell her Tara is the name of the place where the high kings of Ireland lived long ago.

I don't know why I stick my stamps on upside down – I just did it for the laugh the first time, and then I stuck to it, ha ha. I notice you stuck the Queen on upside down on your last letter – I thought you'd get into trouble for that.

You asked if I like carrots. They're OK, I suppose, although I don't know how you can be good with carrots, like you said your mam is. Don't you just boil them until they're soft? That's what we do anyway. Sometimes my mam mashes them up with parsnips, which is OK too. My favourite vegetable is mushy peas. I'd eat them every day if I could.

Must go – teatime,
Luke

PS Almost forgot – Happy Christmas.

ELMA

Elma walked slowly home from school, with Zac and Dylan trailing even more slowly after her. She gave a big, long, feeling-sorry-for-herself sigh. Two and a half weeks till Christmas, and what did she have to look forward to? A big fat nothing – that's what.

That morning Tara had invited her to an early Christmas party in her house. It was going to be on Friday, straight after school. But how could Elma go? Who'd mind the boys?

The more she thought about it, the crosser she got. It just wasn't fair. All the girls in her class were going, even the ones who weren't one bit friendly with Tara. Even the ones who made fun of her London accent behind her back.

It just wasn't fair.

Soon Elma was stamping along the pavement, viciously kicking stones out of her way.

She felt a small hand slip into hers. It was Zac. 'What's wrong, El?' he asked.

Elma gave another big sigh. She didn't usually confide in the boys, but this time she couldn't stop herself. 'I want to go to Tara's party, and I can't.'

Zac squeezed her hand tighter. 'Poor Elma,' he said. 'Didn't she invite you? That's very mean. You should tell your teacher on her.'

Elma stamped her foot so hard it hurt. 'Of course she invited me! She's my best friend! But I can't go, can I?'

Dylan slid alongside her. 'It's because you have to mind us, isn't it?'

Zac smiled brightly. 'But Daddy can mind us.'

Elma and Dylan looked at each other. Poor Zac, too young to realise that their dad could hardly look after himself, much less take care of anyone else. Dylan stood on his tiptoes and whispered into Elma's ear. 'Go to the party. I'll mind Zac until you get home.'

Elma shook her head miserably. 'I couldn't.'

Dylan whispered again. 'Sure you could. Zac and I will be fine. I am nine, you know. We'll walk home, and play quietly until you get back. Dad won't notice, and Mum need never know. You can be back before she gets home.'

Elma looked thoughtfully at her brother. Maybe he was right? It could work. And she deserved to have some fun.

And so she made up her mind.

She was going to the party.

It was the best party she had been to for years. (Actually it was the only party she had been to for years.)

Tara's house was decorated with balloons and ribbons and flashing fairy lights. They had a disco, and a Karaoke competition, and lots of fun games. Then they had pizza and a huge gooey chocolate cake and heaps of sweets.

At seven o'clock, when it was over, and all the other kids had been collected, Tara's mum offered to drive Elma home. That would have been a disaster – imagine if she saw the neglected front garden – imagine if Elma's dad was standing near the window with his stubbly chin, and nothing on besides raggy old tracksuit bottoms and a dirty vest.

So Elma smiled her best smile and said, 'No, thank you. My mum is doing her shopping, and I'm meeting her at the supermarket.'

But no matter how she protested, Tara's mum insisted on driving her to the supermarket, where she had to go in as if she was looking for her mother, hang around until she was sure the coast was clear, and then sneak out and walk all the way home.

She hummed as she walked home, clutching the piece of chocolate cake she'd saved for Zac and Dylan. It had been a lovely afternoon. Just perfect. Maybe she could do it again soon. Maybe she wouldn't have to be the class loser who never went anywhere after all.

She stopped humming as she turned the corner and saw the worst thing ever. She blinked hard, and looked again, but nothing changed – the worst thing ever was still there, parked in the weed-choked driveway. It was her mother's car, all red and shiny and horrible.

Elma checked her watch. It was still only quarter past seven – her mother never got home before half past. Something must have happened.

As she ran up the garden path, Elma had a sick feeling in her stomach that had nothing to do with the three slices of pizza and two pieces of cake she had eaten. She had left the boys with Dad, and gone to Tara's without permission, and now she was in the hugest trouble ever.

The front door was half-open, and her mother was waiting in the hall for her. As she stepped into the light of the hallway, Elma could see that her mother's face was streaked with tears. She had expected shouting and promises of a long grounding, and no treats for about a hundred years. Tears were worse, though. Tears were just too scary.

'What is it, Mum?' she whispered. 'What's going on?'

Her mother shook her head sadly. 'It's not your fault, really it isn't. And he's going to be fine. So you don't have to worry.'

Elma suddenly felt very cold. 'What's not my fault? And who's going to be fine?'

Her mother didn't seem to hear her. 'I won't let them take you into care. I couldn't.'

'Mum, please ... '

Her mother's voice was faint. 'Don't worry. We'll think of something.'

Zac appeared at her side. 'Dylan got hurt. He got burned.'

Elma's breath caught in her throat. 'Where ... where is he?'

'Upstairs.' Zac pointed with an ink-stained finger.

Elma raced up the stairs. Dylan was in bed. All she could see was his pale face, and a huge bandage around his arm.

He gave a weak smile. 'I'm fine, Elma. They gave me a big injection in the hospital, and it doesn't hurt any more.'

Elma sat on the edge of the bed, carefully avoiding Dylan's bandaged arm. 'What happened?'

A big tear rolled down Dylan's pale cheek.

'I'm sorry, Elma. I got you into trouble, didn't I?'
Elma shook her head. 'It doesn't matter. I'm used to being in trouble. Just tell me what happened.'

Dylan wiped his eyes. 'Zac was hungry, and I didn't want him bothering Dad, so I decided to make him some pasta. I always watch you, so I knew what to do. But when I was straining it, the pot slipped, and the hot water went all over my hand, and it hurt like anything. I– '

Elma interrupted. 'Did you call Dad?'

Dylan shook his head. 'I think he was asleep. I told Zac to ring Mum, so he did. And when Mum came, she asked where you were, and I told her you were at Tara's party. I'm sorry, Elma, my hand was hurting and I couldn't think of any lies. Mum wasn't cross with you, though, she just said lots of bad things about Dad. And at the hospital, after I got my bandage, a lady came and asked me and Zac lots of questions.'

'Like what?'

Dylan thought for a minute. 'Like, where was Dad? And why was I making pasta? And why didn't Dad bring me to the hospital? And how did Zac hurt his face that time? And what time did Mum come home every day? And who usually makes the tea? Stuff like that. And then she took Mum into another room, and they talked for ages, and then we all came home. I'm sorry, Elma. I was only trying to help.'

The tears rolled down his face quickly now. 'The lady kept saying something about "alternative arrangements". What does that mean? Does it mean we'll have to go to an orphanage? But we have a mum and dad. We're not orphans. They couldn't make us, could they?'

Elma turned away. How was she supposed to know? What good was a mum who was always at work, and a dad who was always in bed?

She leaned over and wiped Dylan's tears with her sleeve. 'Don't worry, Dyl. It'll be fine. You just wait and see. Here, I brought you some cake.'

Dylan smiled and sat up. Elma felt like crying. If only all their problems could be solved with cake.

She went downstairs. Zac was sitting in the kitchen eating a bowl of cereal. Elma smiled at him. 'There's cake upstairs. Go up and ask Dylan to share with you.'

Zac grinned at her and ran upstairs. Elma looked through the glass door into the family room. The TV was off, so things must be very bad indeed. Her dad was sitting on the couch, and her mum was standing by the door. Elma started to tidy up the kitchen, straining to hear what was going on next door. Soon she didn't have to strain any more, as her parents' voices got louder and louder. After a while she tried not to listen, but she could still hear scraps of sentences.

' … two accidents … bound to ask questions …'

' … not my fault … '

' … they're sending someone around … '

' … they're going to find out the truth, and then we're all in trouble.'

' … my bad back … '

' … get over it!'

After a while, Elma couldn't take it any more. She went upstairs. Zac and Dylan were both asleep in Dylan's bed. She sat on her own bed, and heard the crinkle of Luke Mitchell's latest letter, which was still in her jeans pocket. She pulled it out. She didn't even smile when she saw the upside-down stamp with its candle burning the wrong way up. She wished her penfriend was a girl. Maybe she could have told a girl all her problems. But how could she tell a boy? How could she tell Luke Mitchell what was really going on in her life?

She ripped open the envelope, barely noticing the snowman Luke had drawn on the flap. She read through the letter quickly. All of a sudden, Luke Mitchell sounded like a nicer person – or maybe after what had happened that evening, anyone who wasn't totally horrible would have sounded nice. She wondered why he was so caught up with The Beatles. She really didn't care how many were dead, and what they'd died of. But she wished she hadn't told him so much made-up stuff. She was tired of writing lies about vegetables and cookery books and non-existent sisters and a cuddly cat that was really a vicious dog. It would have been nice to tell Luke all about Dylan's arm, and her mum's three jobs, and how she was so worried about the future. But there were so many lies that she didn't know how to go about setting them right.

Then she had a thought. She reached under her bed and took out the Christmas card she'd made for her mother. She rubbed her finger along the glittery pink and purple star. She looked at the swirly Happy Christmas that she'd carefully written on the inside. She decided that her mum didn't deserve such a nice card. Her dad was sick; he couldn't help it that he was useless. But her mum wasn't sick, and she was the adult. She should sort things out. She should be there so Elma could go to parties without leaving her brothers to mind themselves. She started to cry at how unfair it all was. Tears dripped down her face and onto the glittery star, making it slightly soggy. Then Elma picked up her pen and wrote inside the card:

To dear Luke,

Have a happy Christmas, from Elma.

She shoved the card into its envelope, addressed it, and stuck on her stamp (upside down of course). Then she tore a page from an old copy, and watched as yet more lies flowed from her pen.

Dear Luke,

Thanks for your letter. I've kind of got used to the upside-down stamps by now. Maybe we'll start a new fashion.

I was just kidding about The Beatles. Of course I knew they weren't all dead.

I don't like soccer all that much. Lots of days I play basketball after school, though. (That's when I'm not playing the violin or going to ballet lessons or just hanging out with Tara.)

I'm really looking forward to Christmas. Jessica is too young to understand, but I've bought her lots of lovely presents already. My favourite is the life-sized doll who cries real tears. I've bought a lovely new cat bed for Snowball. It's made of soft, pink furry stuff and I know she's going to love it.

Have you bought nice presents for your mum and dad and your sisters and your granny? At least you'll have lots of money from your car-washing job.

Tara had a great party today. I was going to sleep over, but then I decided to go home instead because Mum and Dad promised to take me bowling. Actually Mum's calling me now, so gotta go.

Have a Coooool Christmas.
Hope you like the card,
Elma

LUKE

He lifted the custard tin down from the shelf in the wardrobe and eased off the metal lid. When he held it upside down over his bed, a shower of coins and notes tumbled out. He made separate bundles of the five and ten euro notes, and arranged the coins in neat towers on top of his chest of drawers.

Then, pretending he didn't know exactly how much he had, he counted it all carefully.

Four hundred and ten euro. One euro more than the washing machine cost – and tomorrow, Monday, was Christmas Eve. Luke was going in first thing in the morning to buy it. He wondered if they'd be able to deliver it tomorrow, or if he'd have to wait till after Christmas.

Not that it mattered really. The main thing was that he'd made it. He'd saved enough to buy the washing machine that was going to make his mother happy. He couldn't wait to see her face when she saw it.

Pity he wouldn't be able to buy anyone else anything, though. He'd just have to tell them that their presents would be a bit late this year, that's all.

Not that they'd gone in for making much of a fuss at Christmas, since the accident. The first year, when Dad was still in the hospital, they hadn't even got a tree. Uncle Jack and Aunt Maureen had invited them all out to the farm for Christmas dinner, but Mam said no, they'd be better off at home.

So she cooked a turkey like she always did, and Granny, who had been coming to them at Christmas for years anyway, made mince pies like she always did. And they pulled crackers and watched the same films they always watched, and Luke wondered if he was the only one who missed Dad desperately.

In the afternoon, Mam and Helen and Granny went to the hospital with presents. Helen's eyes were red when she came home.

Luke didn't think Helen would be buying anyone any presents this year. She still wasn't really talking to anyone in the house, except her grandmother when nobody else was there. If Luke walked into the room, she'd stop straightaway.

She still wasn't allowed out during the week, and she had to be in by ten on Friday and Saturday, and nine on Sunday. She told nobody where she was going, or who she'd be with. When she was at home, she still spent most of the time in her room.

She never talked to her father these days, or sat with him like she used to when he came home first. The only time she saw him now was at tea, and then she ignored him like she ignored everyone else, staying just long enough to pick at what was on her plate before disappearing upstairs again.

Anne would hardly be getting presents for anyone either – as soon as she got the five euro that Granny gave her every Friday, she spent it on comics that kept her busy till Monday, and then she traded them at school for more comics that looked exactly the same to Luke, with a picture of some teenage pop star on the cover, and headlines like 'Make Your Own Bracelets' or 'Ten Signs of a True Friend' and sometimes a free packet of stickers or a lip gloss attached to the front.

Anne read each comic from cover to cover, and filled in all the puzzle pages, and read everybody's horoscope out loud at teatime, even Helen's.

Anne was still a bit wary of Dad. She didn't like

being left in a room alone with him, even if he was only sitting in his armchair looking out the window, or gazing at the television. She'd shoot quick glances at him across the table at tea when she thought nobody was looking, when he was opening his mouth to let Mam's fork in, or chewing noisily, or lifting his water glass with a hand that shook so much you were waiting for it to come tumbling down.

Of course Granny would buy Christmas presents – or make them. Last year Luke got a blue scarf and gloves, and Helen and Anne both got hats with pompoms. Mam got perfume and Dad got a scarf like Luke's, but in green.

And Mam would make sure everyone had something, even if it was a much smaller something than they'd got in the past, when Dad was working. Last year she gave each of the three children a selection box and €20. She gave Granny three scratchcards and a box of fudge. Granny won ten euro on one of the cards and bought five more, but won nothing the second time.

Nobody really knew what to get Dad for Christmas now. He didn't read any more, except for bits of the daily paper when he was in the mood, so the book tokens he'd always loved were no good.

He never listened to music any more either, and

didn't seem to notice if Luke put on a Beatles or Supertramp CD. He rarely went out, apart from when his brother Jack collected him and took him to the farm for the afternoon, or when Mam drove him to the doctor or the hospital for a check-up, so any kind of shopping voucher was useless.

He didn't really do *anything* any more – and he could eat only so many of his favourite fruit pastilles. Last year he ended up with three boxes of them.

Luke hadn't given him pastilles – he'd given him a 100-piece jigsaw, which was still sitting on a shelf in the sitting room, unopened. Mam explained to Luke that his father's concentration was gone, that he wouldn't be able to keep his attention on the jigsaw, but Luke felt he could at least have tried.

Before he went upstairs to bed that evening, he asked his mother to call him when she was leaving for work in the morning.

She looked surprised. 'You don't want a lie-in, on Christmas Eve?'

'Nah – I've stuff to do.'

She gave a tiny smile and turned back to the TV screen. 'About half eight so?'

'Yeah, thanks. Night.'

'Goodnight, love. Sleep tight.'

Luke left the sitting room and tiptoed into his

father's room next door. There was a faint glow from the nightlight in the corner, enough for Luke to make out the hump of his father's body under the bedclothes. The room was hot, and smelt of toothpaste.

Luke sat in the chair beside the bed. His father's eyes were closed, and his breathing was quick and shallow, like a small child's, with a little wheeze at the end of every in-breath. One of his hands lay palm up on the pillow beside his head. From next door Luke could still hear the muffled sound of the TV.

He reached over and laid his hand gently, palm to palm, on his father's. He felt the warm breath coming from his father's mouth. He watched the tiny lift and fall of the bedclothes. He stroked his father's cheek lightly, felt the roughness of the stubble.

He whispered 'Dad', too softly to be heard.

His father's breathing didn't change. Luke sat back in the chair and watched, and pretended.

When his father was asleep, pretending was easier. Pretending that the birthday party hadn't even happened on that horrible day, or that Luke had got sick and couldn't go. Or that Mam had a day off from work and came to bring him home instead of Dad, and stopped at all the red lights on the way home.

Pretending that when Dad woke up, he'd look at

Luke and ruffle his hair and say, 'How's my son and heir?' just like he used to.

Just like nothing had ever happened to him.

After a few minutes, Luke tiptoed from the room and went upstairs to bed.

He was waiting outside Brady's Electrical when it opened at half past nine the next morning. The woman who unlocked the door looked at him.

'Hello there.' She glanced up the street behind him. 'Are you all on your own?'

'I want to buy a washing machine,' Luke said. 'That one.' He pointed to the window.

She followed his finger, then looked back at him doubtfully. 'You know how much it costs?'

'Four hundred and nine euro,' Luke told her, wondering why she couldn't see the price written clearly on the top. 'Can you deliver it today?'

She smiled. 'First things first,' she said. 'Come on in.' As Luke followed her into the shop, she asked, 'Is it a present?'

'Yeah,' Luke said. 'A surprise, for my mother.'

She stopped and looked back at him. 'Did you save all the money yourself?'

Luke nodded. Then he thought maybe she didn't believe him, so he pulled the bulky brown envelope out of his pocket and held it out to her.

She didn't take it, just looked at it in his hand for a few seconds. Then she gave a quick look around the shop and said, more softly, 'You know, this isn't a good time to buy a washing machine.'

It wasn't what Luke was expecting to hear. He lowered the envelope slowly. 'Why not?'

He had no idea that it mattered *when* you bought a washing machine. Didn't people wash clothes all year round?

'Because our sale is starting on Friday,' the woman explained. 'And that washing machine will be reduced by fifteen percent.' She turned towards a nearby desk. 'Here – I'll tell you how much you'll save if you can wait till then.'

Luke watched as she tapped numbers into a calculator. Then she turned back to him.

'Sixty-one euro and thirty-five cents,' she said. 'That's how much cheaper it'll be on Friday.'

Luke thought quickly. He could buy pretty good presents for everyone with sixty euro – and Mam would still have her machine, just a few days later. Then he thought of something.

'What if someone else comes in today and buys it?' he asked. It wouldn't be much good reducing the price of a machine that wasn't there any more.

'You can pay me a deposit,' the woman explained.

'And I'll hold it for you.' She winked at Luke. 'Just don't tell anyone, because we're not supposed to do that for the sales. Make sure you look for me when you come back on Friday to pay the balance, OK?' She pointed to the nametag pinned to her blouse. 'Look for Jenny.'

Ten minutes later, Luke left the shop with three hundred and sixty euro in his envelope, and a receipt for the fifty euro he'd given Jenny to make sure the washing machine would still be there on Friday.

He bought an annual for Anne, a HMV voucher for Helen, a pair of slippers for Dad, a box of perfumed drawer liners for Granny and a gift set of hand cream and body lotion for Mam. He wouldn't mention the washing machine until Friday.

On the way home he went into the newsagents and bought a Happy New Year card and a stamp. He felt a bit guilty that he hadn't sent a Christmas card to his penfriend – even though the one she sent him was no great shakes, all crinkled and messy looking when he pulled it out of the envelope, and loads of little sparkly bits falling off it onto his jeans. She must have used too much glue or something. But at least she'd made the effort.

After tea he wrapped all his presents with the roll of shiny red paper he'd bought. Then he hid them under his bed and took out the card. It had a bunch of flowers on the front – she'd probably like that.

For the first time, he wondered what she looked like. She'd never said anything about that. He tried to remember how he'd described himself in his first letter. Black hair with blue tips, wasn't it? Something about tattoos – and didn't he say he had something pierced, his nose or eyebrow or something?

Just as well his penfriend hadn't asked for his photo, because absolutely none of that was true. His hair was muddy brown, not black at all, with no coloured tips, and he definitely had no tattoos or earrings – Mam would go mad if he tried anything like that.

And all the stuff about Dad being an astronaut, and Helen a model, and the rubbish about the racehorses – and didn't he tell her they lived in a big fancy house with a lake out the back? He wondered what she'd say if she ever found out the truth.

He wished he knew for sure if she made anything up when she wrote to him – how would he ever know? Her life could be totally different, like his was.

He licked the stamp and stuck it the right way up on the envelope – just for fun, just to see if she'd notice. Then he opened the card and began to write.

Dear Penfriend,

I hope you had a good Christmas. I haven't had any Christmas yet – it's still Christmas Eve. Today I went shopping and bought presents for all the family. I don't like shopping too much, so I got them all in about half an hour, but I think they'll like them.

~~I've got a big surprise for my Mam~~ Do they have the same Christmas dinner in England as we have here? We always have a turkey and two kinds of potatoes, mashed and roast, and Brussels sprouts, which I'm not mad about, and my granny makes mince pies for dessert, and we put custard on them. Most people have plum pudding for dessert on Christmas Day, but nobody in the family likes that.

Oh, and we just make gravy out of stuff in a big tub that you mix with boiling water.

Well, I better go to sleep – I'm wrecked.

Luke

PS Thanks for your card. Hope you like this one – all my own work, ha ha.

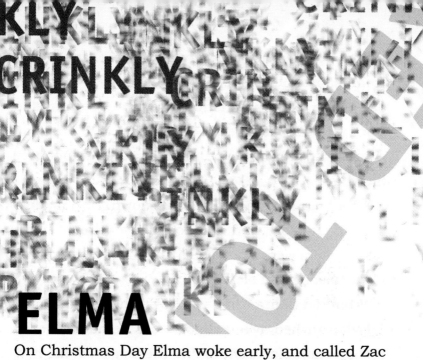

ELMA

On Christmas Day Elma woke early, and called Zac and Dylan, and they all ran downstairs together to open their presents. It didn't take long. She got a book and a crinkly red top. She'd already read the book about two years earlier, and when she tried on the top, it was so small that one of the seams ripped. Their mother came in as Zac and Dylan opened a big pile of packages that turned out to contain Pokemon figures. Dylan looked kind of sulky, and Zac started to cry. He looked at his mother. 'Why didn't Santa know that Dylan and me don't play with Pokemon any more?' he wailed.

Elma thought her mum was going to cry, too, but she turned away quickly, and went into the kitchen.

Elma hugged her brothers and gave them each a small chocolate reindeer she'd bought for them the day before. 'Happy Christmas, guys,' she said, as she wondered if there was any hope of Christmas actually turning out to be anything other than totally horrible.

After breakfast their dad came down. He'd made a kind of an effort, and had actually got dressed, but his trousers were all creased, and his jumper looked like someone had slept in it.

'What did Santa bring you boys?' he asked.

Dylan turned away, almost as if he hadn't heard the question. Zac went to find the biggest of his new Pokemon. By then, though, their dad had walked into the TV room, and was already engrossed in a programme about baby turtles.

Elma helped her mum to tidy up the kitchen, and then everyone went to sit in the TV room. The first row was because Dad refused to allow the TV to be switched to anything besides the National Geographic Channel.

The second row was because Zac, who didn't really understand what was wrong, was trying to make things better by loudly and enthusiastically playing with his unwanted toys. This was fine for about a minute and a half, until Dad started shouting at Zac for being so noisy, and Mum started shouting at Dad for being so mean, and Zac cried softly, and Dylan sat in a corner with a white face and said nothing at all.

The third row was over a box of chocolates, and after that, Elma stopped counting. The day dragged slowly on, with short periods of calm divided up by bouts of loud shouting.

Dinner was OK – if you just ate the slices of turkey that didn't have any of Mum's lumpy gravy on them. While the rest of the family was fighting over the last soggy potato, Elma sneaked her plate into the back yard and fed the brown-covered bits to Snowball. Snowball didn't seem to mind and even wagged his tail a bit. Elma was glad that at least someone was happy. She patted him and was rewarded with a big puff of gravy-breath.

Even though she was allowed to stay up as late as she liked, Elma went to bed at ten. Bed was less scary than listening to all those fights. As she lay there with her eyes closed, she realised why the day had been so bad – it was the first day in a very long time that her mum had spent at home. For the first day in ages and ages, her mum had no work to go to, and with a jolt of sadness, Elma understood that the biggest problem of all was that her parents could no longer bear to be together.

Boxing Day was nearly as bad as the day before, and after that things began to get a bit better, as Elma's mum left the house more and more to go to work. Elma wondered what kind of offices needed cleaning two days after Christmas. Was her mum like the woman she'd seen on TV once, who left her house every morning pretending to go to work, but really spent her time hanging around parks and shopping centres?

One morning, about four days after Christmas, when her mum was gone out, and the boys were playing in their bedroom, Elma decided it was time to talk to her dad. She waited for an ad-break, and then pounced. Before he could react, she switched off the television and ran to sit beside her dad.

'Dad,' she said in her gentlest voice. 'Why don't you go back to work?'

He looked at her, and she tried to ignore his wrinkled top and his unshaven chin. He gave a big sigh. 'You know I can't work, love. I'll never work again.'

· Elma took a deep breath. 'The doctor said you'll never work *as a plumber* again. But you could do something else.'

'Like what?'

Elma sighed. How was she supposed to know stuff

like that? 'I don't know, Dad. But you could find out. Why don't you get dressed, and we could go and look in the window of the job centre?'

'But–'

Elma ignored him. 'We could bring Snowball. He'd love the walk.'

Elma thought she'd die if anyone saw her in public with Snowball, but it would be worth it if it got Dad out of the house.

For a moment she thought she could see a flicker of life in her father's eyes, then it faded as quickly as it had come. He reached for the remote control. 'Thanks, love,' he said. 'I'm a bit tired today. Maybe we'll do it next week. Now turn the TV back on, there's a good girl.'

Elma stamped out of the room, slamming the door behind her. She felt like crying, or screaming, or something, but what was the point? It wouldn't change anything. Then she punched the wall anyway, just because she couldn't think of anything else to do.

The bruise lasted for eight days.

Elma trudged into school after the holidays, with Zac and Dylan trailing behind her. She felt sorry for them, of course she did, but she felt sorry for herself, too, and what good did that do her?

As soon as she walked into the classroom, Evil Josh came over. 'Did you have a nice Christmas?' he asked. 'Did you get lots of lovely lumpy gravy every day? Did your dad have any more stupid accidents?'

Elma felt like hitting him, but she didn't fancy a day sitting in the headmaster's office, so she resisted, and walked away, biting her tongue.

Just then Tara came in. She raced over to Elma and hugged her. 'Elma, great to see you,' she said. 'Did you have the best Christmas ever? I so did. I got the best presents. I got an Ipod with the coolest skin ever, and a big box of make-up, and a whole new outfit, oh and loads of other stuff. And me and my family went ice-skating, and bowling, and we went to the panto, and ... '

She kept talking, but Elma stopped listening. She didn't want to be mean to her friend, but it was just too awful. Why couldn't she have a nice life like Tara?

Just then Mrs Lawrence came in, clutching a bundle of envelopes.

'Settle down, children,' she said. 'Now, here are your letters from Ireland, and since it's the first day back, I am going to allow you to read them, and reply at once.'

Elma took her envelope and examined it. For once

Luke Mitchell had managed to stick his stamp the right way up. In a way she was disappointed. She opened the envelope and pulled out a Happy New Year card. It didn't seem like the kind of card Luke would buy. Maybe his mum had bought it for him? She sighed as she read what he'd written inside. *His* Christmas dinner sounded really good.

But she wished he wouldn't keep going on about gravy. What had she been thinking of, telling him her mum was writing a book about gravy? The book her mum should have written was *How to Turn your Back on your Family and Pretend not to Notice that it was Falling Apart.*

Elma struggled to read a bit that for some reason Luke had crossed out. Something about a surprise for his mum. She wondered why he'd crossed it out. Then she looked around and noticed that everyone else had already started their letters, so she pulled out a sheet of paper and began to write.

Dear Luke,

I had a really awful Christmas. My mum and dad were fighting all the time, and my brothers spent most of the time hiding in their bedroom. My mum is the worst cook in the world, and I was glad when she went back to work so we didn't have to eat lumpy gravy any more. Snowball is really a—

Just then Elma heard Mrs Lawrence coming up behind her desk. She jumped up, ran to the waste paper basket, and shredded her letter into tiny, fluttery little pieces. She smiled at Mrs Lawrence as she went back to her seat. 'I made a spelling mistake,' she said. Then she got a new piece of paper, and began again.

Dear Luke,

I had the best Christmas ever. I got an Ipod with a cool pink skin, and a big box of make-up, and great new jeans and a jumper and loads of other things. Me and my family did the coolest stuff. We went ice-skating and bowling, and to a panto. (That was a bit boring but Jessica seemed to love it – she kept clapping even when she was meant to be quiet, and the woman in front of us was very cross.)

Snowball loves her new bed, and she spends most of her day lying in it, purring.

In our house we have plum pudding on Christmas Day. Dad pours brandy on it, and sets it on fire, and then we all sing 'We Wish You a Merry Christmas' until the flames go out. It's great fun. (But not as much fun as eating the pudding. It's always totally yummy.)

I hope you got nice presents. Did you get a new horse to replace Rocket yet? I suppose Santa would find it hard to get a horse down the chimney (ha ha).

Why didn't you put your stamp on upside down this time?

Bye and Happy New Year,
Elma

LUKE

One bit of sky was still missing. Luke pointed to the gap.

'Look, Dad, we need a blue piece here, OK?'

His father looked down at the half-finished scene on the table. 'We need a blue piece here, OK,' he said. He scanned the scattered jigsaw pieces. 'We need a blue piece here, OK.' He picked up a piece that was mostly green with a tiny bit of blue in one corner and held it out to Luke. 'OK?'

It was clearly not the bit they needed, but Luke took it and tried to fit it in. 'No, that's not it. We need another one.' But just then a dog began to bark outside, and his father's head swung towards the window.

Luke found another three pieces and fitted them into their places, and then he pushed back his chair and stood up. 'Let's do some more later, OK?' As if the two of them were doing it together.

His father nodded, still turned towards the window. 'Do some more later, OK?'

In the kitchen Luke's mother finished loading the two-week-old washing machine and straightened up. 'OK, love?'

'Yeah.' Luke watched her pressing the buttons, twirling the temperature knob. A second later he heard the gush of water as the cycle began. Funny how he thought something like a new washing machine could make anyone happy. It hadn't changed things at all, this shiny new thing in the corner of the kitchen. His mother still looked tired and sad most of the time. Helen still went around with what Granny called a face as long as a wet week. His father – well, of course his father hadn't changed. And Anne was still bringing her bundled-up sheets downstairs at least twice a week.

And the worst thing of all was that they didn't even own the washing machine, not properly. They wouldn't own it for another six months, because of what happened to Luke the day he went to buy it.

Christmas had gone pretty well, considering.

There hadn't been any rows between Helen and Mam, and everyone had actually got a present for everyone else, even if Helen only managed a chocolate bar each – Luke got an Aero – and Anne's presents were poems for everyone. This was what she wrote about Luke:

My big brother is cool
He goes to my school
His hair is dark, he's like a shark,
He likes playing in the park.

Luke thought it was actually pretty good for a seven-year-old. Anne had written the poem out carefully in purple ink and stuck different coloured stars all around it.

This year, Granny had given each of the three children a ten-euro book token. Mam got clothes for everyone – a sweatshirt for Luke, a skirt for Anne and a top for Helen.

Luke's father, of course, didn't give out any presents. He watched as the others were being distributed, a half smile on his face. When he was handed something he took it with a look of faint surprise and held it in his lap until Mam or Granny opened it for him, and then put it somewhere else.

Everyone loved Luke's presents. Even Helen smiled slightly when she opened the envelope and pulled out the HMV voucher.

'Thanks, Lukey.' She hadn't called him Lukey in ages. Hadn't called him anything in ages.

His father looked down at his new slippers, and then put a hand briefly on Luke's arm. 'Yeah,' he said. 'Nice, yeah.'

Anne gave a scream of delight when she saw her new annual, and then threw her arms around Luke. 'Thank you sooo much, Lukey, it's brilliant.' Granny told him the drawer liners were just what she always wanted, and Mam hugged him tightly when he gave her the body lotion and hand cream, and whispered, 'Thanks, love'.

And all through the dinner, and afterwards, when they were sitting in front of the telly (except for Helen, who'd gone upstairs, and Dad, who was having a nap), Luke kept thinking about getting the new washing machine, and imagining Mam's face when she saw it.

On Friday morning he'd lain in bed, waiting for the day to start. As soon as he heard Mam getting up for work he dressed quickly, shivering in the icy bedroom air, and followed her downstairs.

She looked up in surprise as he walked into the

kitchen. 'What are you up so early for?'

'I need to get something in town.' He waited for her to ask what – he was dying to say 'a surprise' – but she just nodded.

'Have a bit of breakfast and you can come in with me.'

It was nice to have her to himself. Usually Granny was around, or Anne. He took two slices of bread from the loaf and dropped them into the toaster. 'You know my penfriend?' he said.

'The girl in England?' Mam was spreading marmalade on her toast.

Luke nodded. 'They have plum pudding for Christmas, and they pour brandy on it and set it on fire.'

Mam didn't look surprised, like he thought she would. 'A lot of people do that,' she said. 'I just think it's a waste of brandy.'

'Yeah.' Luke thought for a minute, watching the inside of the toaster getting red. 'I made up a few things when I started to write to her first,' he said.

'You did?' Mam looked across the kitchen at him. 'Like what?'

Luke shrugged, feeling her eyes on him. 'Oh just … that I had a tattoo, and blue hair, and stuff.' He paused. 'And that Dad was a famous astronaut, and

112

that we had a big house with loads of horses, and a lake in the back garden.' The bread was turning golden.

'Why did you say all that?' Mam didn't sound cross, just curious.

Luke began to be sorry he'd started. 'I dunno ... maybe because I didn't want ... ' he paused, not sure how to put it. Then he said, 'I didn't want her to feel sorry for me.'

Mam picked up her toast and took a bite. She chewed it slowly, and when she'd swallowed it she said, 'You mean about Dad.'

Luke nodded, wishing he could go back a few sentences and keep his mouth closed. The toast popped up suddenly, startling him.

'You miss him, don't you?' Mam's voice was very gentle.

The tears in his eyes took him by surprise. He blinked them away quickly and lifted the toast out and brought it over to the table.

'It's OK – I miss him too,' Mam said, as he sat across from her. She put a hand on Luke's. 'But you shouldn't be ashamed of what happened – it wasn't your fault.'

A tear slid down Luke's cheek and plopped onto the table. He pulled his hand away from hers and wiped roughly at his eyes. 'If the party wasn't on–'

'Don't think like that.' Mam interrupted him loudly. 'Stop thinking like that. The party had nothing to do with it, nothing. Dad could have been coming from anywhere, and it could still have happened.' Then she said in a softer voice, 'OK?'

'OK.' Luke began to spread butter on his toast, struggling to keep more tears from falling. How had this conversation happened? He should never have mentioned his penfriend. He wished with all his heart that Mrs Hutchinson had never come up with the idea of getting penfriends for them.

He took a deep breath and then looked back at Mam with what he hoped was a fairly cheerful face. 'OK.' And for the rest of the breakfast neither of them mentioned Dad, or penfriends.

When Mam stood up to go, Luke said, 'Hang on a sec,' and ran upstairs. He shoved the receipt for the deposit he'd paid on the washing machine into his jeans pocket, and the brown envelope with the money into the pocket of his jacket. It made a rectangular bulge that he hoped Mam wouldn't notice. As he ran downstairs again he tried to remember the name of the woman in the shop – Jennifer? Jane? Something that began with 'J' anyway. He was pretty sure he'd remember her when he saw her.

Mam dropped him outside the cinema. 'Are you sure this is OK?'

Luke nodded. The cinema was about ten minutes' walk from Brady's Electrical, past a hospital and an office block, through a little park and around by some flats. 'See you at home,' he told his mother, and walked off.

It was a chilly day. Luke walked quickly, his jacket tightly buttoned and his hands jammed into the pockets. His left hand was wrapped around the bulky envelope. His breath fogged out in front of him. He passed the hospital and the offices, and turned into the park.

It was quiet there. Luke guessed that anyone who didn't have to go to work today was still tucked up in bed. The few trees he passed were bare and cold looking. The flowerbeds were empty and brown, no sign of snowdrops yet. The two swings in the little play area hung silently, no wind to move them. Luke kicked at a stone, watched it skip along ahead of him before coming to rest at the feet of another boy, who stood on the path facing Luke.

He looked a bit older, although it was hard to see him properly, with the grey hood of his sweatshirt covering his head, and a black scarf knotted tightly around his neck and chin. Taller than Luke, too, and thinner. He stood watching as Luke got nearer, not making any attempt to move out of his way.

Luke began to swerve around him, but the other boy put out a hand and jammed it into Luke's chest. 'Give us your phone.' His other hand pointed towards the bulge in Luke's left pocket. 'C'mon.'

Luke's heart thumped. He tried to pull away, but the boy's fist was wrapped tightly around the front of Luke's jacket. He snapped the fingers of his other hand. 'Your phone – c'mon,' he said, a bit louder now. 'Give us it.'

'I haven't got a phone,' Luke said, hating the tremble in his voice. In his pocket, his hand gripped the envelope tightly.

The boy swore loudly, and reached towards Luke's pocket. 'Give us here.' He grabbed Luke's left arm and began trying to yank Luke's hand out of the pocket. He wore a thin leather wristband.

Luke knew it was useless – he'd have to try and fool the boy. He pulled out the envelope and held it up. 'It's not a phone, look. It's just – a letter.'

It happened so fast: the boy grabbed the envelope, and pushed Luke backwards before racing away. Luke fell onto the grass and watched him, knowing he hadn't a hope of catching him, or getting back the envelope even if he did. His heart was thumping painfully in his chest, and one of his wrists hurt from trying to break his fall. He put his head in his hands and sat on the grass, shaking. His money, every cent he'd saved, was gone. The washing machine was gone. It was all over.

After a few minutes he stood up. He had no idea if he'd get his deposit back, but he may as well try. All they could say was no. His legs still trembled a bit as he walked slowly through the park and towards Brady's Electrical. The main street was busier than he'd expected – most of the shop windows had big 'Sale' signs in them. He hoped he wouldn't meet anyone he knew.

There were quite a few in Brady's, but he spotted the woman straight away, talking to a couple in the corner. She noticed him after he'd been standing there for a few minutes, and signalled him to wait. Luke leant against a wall and wondered what she'd say when he told her he couldn't buy the washing machine after all. Would she be cross, after holding on to it for him? After telling him they didn't usually let people put deposits on things during the sale?

Jenny wasn't cross. She put her hands to her cheeks as Luke told her what had happened. Then she took him into a little room behind the shop and sat him down and poured him a glass of warm orange juice from a carton. She asked him if he was hurt, and if he'd reported the mugging to the police. She told him to wait there, and then she went away for what seemed like a long time.

Luke poured the juice carefully back into the carton – he thought he'd probably throw up if he drank it. His wrist ached, and he couldn't seem to stop shivering, although it was warm in the little room.

Did Jenny believe him? Maybe she thought he'd changed his mind about buying the washing machine, and now he was just trying to get his money back. Maybe she was ringing the police to come and take him away for lying. Maybe Mam would have to come and collect him from the police station, like she'd collected him from the hospital the day everything changed.

But when Jenny came back, she was alone. She pulled a chair over and sat beside Luke.

'Now, I've had a word with the boss,' she told Luke. 'He thinks it's awful, what happened to you, and he says you can still get the washing machine, on interest-free credit, if you want.'

Luke looked at her. 'What's that?' he asked. It sounded complicated.

'It means that instead of paying for it all today, like you were going to, you can pay a bit every month until you've paid the full amount,' Jenny explained. 'That's called credit. Interest free means that you won't pay anything extra, just what it costs.'

It sounded promising. Luke did some fast calculating. Jack gave him sixty euro a month, and he'd make at least another twenty from washing cars. 'How much would I have to pay?' he asked.

Jenny looked down at the pad she held. 'Fifty euro a month,' she said, 'for six months.' She looked back at Luke. 'How does that sound?'

'Fine.' So Mam would have to wait six months for her new machine – but it was a lot better than not getting it at all. Just as well Luke hadn't said anything about it at home.

'One more thing.' Jenny paused. 'You can't sign the credit agreement – it has to be a person over eighteen. Now I know you want it to be a surprise for your mam, so how about your dad? Could he come in and sign for you?'

Luke shook his head, his heart sinking. He might have known it was too good to be true. 'He had an accident,' he told Jenny. 'He's – he never goes out any more.' He didn't tell her that Dad hadn't written a word since the accident, couldn't write his name now. 'Maybe I could get my granny … ' he began uncertainly. How would Granny feel about signing?

Jenny was watching him carefully. 'I'll tell you what,' she said. 'I'll sign, if you like.'

Luke looked at her. 'You?' He wasn't sure how big a deal it was, signing a credit agreement for someone, but he guessed it was pretty big. Especially when you didn't know the person you were signing for. Especially when the person was just a kid.

'I'll sign,' Jenny told him. 'I have a feeling about you. I don't think you'll let me down.' Then she smiled. 'And even if you do, I could use a new washing machine myself.'

For the first time since the bad thing in the park, Luke felt his heart lifting. 'Thank you,' he said. It didn't sound like enough, but he couldn't think what else to say.

They went back out to the shop and Jenny went through the form with him. When they'd finished, she said, 'Right then – how does this afternoon suit?'

Luke looked at her. 'For what?' Was there something else he had to do?

Jenny smiled. 'To deliver the washing machine, of course. You do want it, don't you?'

'Today?' Luke couldn't believe it. 'I thought we wouldn't get it until I paid the full amount.'

Jenny shook her head. 'Sorry, Luke – I thought you knew that. As soon as you sign up and pay the deposit – which you've already done – you get the goods. Will there be someone at home this afternoon to take it in?'

And so, just after half past four, a white van pulled up outside the house. When Luke answered the door, a man in blue overalls stood there with the new washing machine on a trolley. And by the time everything was explained to Granny, and after the man had installed the new machine and was wheeling out the old one, Mam arrived home from work.

She got out of the car and walked over to the van, frowning. 'Oh no, don't tell me it's packed up.'

The man looked from Mam to Luke. 'Will you tell her, or will I?'

Luke suddenly felt shy. He wished the man wasn't there. He said, 'I got you a new one. It's inside.' This wasn't how he'd planned it.

Mam's hand flew to her mouth. For a minute she just stood there, saying nothing. The man finished loading up the old machine and grinned at Mam's face as he opened the driver's door. 'Maybe you should go in and have a look, Missus. All the best now, Happy New Year.' He climbed in, slammed the door and drove off.

Luke and Mam were left standing in the driveway. At last, Mam took down her hand. 'A new washing machine?' she asked. Her voice sounded odd.

Luke couldn't figure out if she was happy or annoyed. 'Come in and see it.'

In the kitchen, Mam crouched down in front of the new machine and examined all the knobs and buttons very carefully. Luke stood beside Granny and watched, afraid to say anything.

Then Mam stood up slowly and turned around, and her face still had that strange expression on it. 'How much did it cost?' She spoke softly.

'I got it in the sale,' Luke said. 'It wasn't too dear.' Was she angry with him?

'How did you get the money?'

'I saved it up.' No way was he telling her what happened in the park.

Then Mam went over and put her arms around Luke, and he could feel her crying, and she whispered, 'Oh my God, what are you like? What did I do to deserve you?' And he knew she wasn't angry with him.

For the next few days, the new washing machine was the centre of attention in the house – Dad even came into the kitchen especially to see it. And then, gradually, everyone forgot about it, and stopped talking about Luke's big surprise, and Mam yelled at Helen for giving her cheek, and Granny tried to keep the peace, and Dad put his head in his hands and rocked himself, and moaned quietly.

Luke didn't tell anyone about the bad thing in the park. Jenny in the shop was the only person who knew. What could anyone do about it, if he told them? It would only worry them, and there was enough to worry about in the house.

He didn't think there was any hope of the police finding the boy and getting the money back, since Luke hadn't even seen his face properly. All he could remember was the boy's grey hoodie and black scarf, and the thin leather band he wore around his wrist. There must be hundreds of boys wearing exactly the same stuff.

But the longer he kept the bad thing inside him, the harder it got not to tell someone. It was like a kind of balloon, getting bigger and bigger, waiting to burst apart some day unless he let the air out.

And then, two weeks after the washing machine arrived, just a few days after he went back to school, he got a letter from his penfriend.And as he was reading about her too-good-to-be-true family, and the perfect Christmas she'd had, he suddenly thought: *I could tell her. I could tell her what happened in the park.* She wouldn't be able to tell anyone in his family. And this time, it was all perfectly true.

But maybe he'd dress it up a bit, just to make him sound less pathetic.

He thought it was a bit rude of her not to mention the New Year card he'd sent. But maybe she was ashamed, because her card was homemade, and not half as nice as his.

He wrote the address on the envelope and stuck his stamp on upside down again. He didn't really care any more, but she seemed to like it. He sucked the end of his biro for a few minutes, and then he picked up his notebook.

Dear Penfriend,

Isn't it great being back at school? (Ha ha.) I had an exciting holiday. A few days after Christmas I was mugged in a park by a gang of much older boys and all my money was stolen, almost three hundred euro. (I don't know what that is in English money, but it's a lot.)

I was going to buy a new washing machine for my mam as a surprise. Anyway, the gang took it all, and hurt my hand too. I'm OK now. And my mam still got the washing machine, because the shop said I could pay a bit every month instead. In six months it'll be all paid for.

The police are looking for the gang now. I was able to give really good descriptions, so hopefully they'll catch them and get back my money.

My mam thinks pouring brandy on a pudding is a waste of money. I think it's cool, eating something that's on fire. Maybe we'll set Granny's mince pies on fire next year, ha ha.

It's my birthday next week. I'll be twelve years and no months old. Or else I'll be one hundred and forty-four months old. My granny is baking my favourite chocolate biscuit cake. She puts in marshmallows and cherries and nuts and really cool stuff. Maybe she should write a book about baking cakes – she makes excellent ones.

Bye for now,
Luke
PS Let's stop talking about stamps. It's too boring.

ELMA

The first time Mrs Clifford called, Zac opened the front door. Probably not a good idea, as at the time he was wearing only his underpants and a t-shirt with a trail of baked beans dripping down the front. Elma ran into the hall, to see who was at the door. Mrs Clifford was talking to Zac, but it was difficult to hear what she was saying, as Dad had turned the TV up to its full volume.

Elma felt at once that the arrival of the smartly dressed stranger could only mean trouble. She ran to her dad and hissed in his ear. 'Turn down the TV, quick. There's a woman at the door.'

Dad grunted. 'Get rid of her.'

Elma crossed the room and switched off the TV. 'I

don't think I can. Just tidy yourself up a bit. Quick.'

She went back into the hall, and smiled nervously at the stranger. The stranger smiled back. 'My name is Mrs Clifford. I'm from Social Services. Can I speak to your mother or your father, please?'

By now Dylan had appeared in the hallway. He was standing next to his brother, with a tear-stained face. They'd had another of their mega-rows over whose turn it was to heat up the baked beans for tea.

Elma smiled again, as if a smile would distract Mrs Clifford from the state of her brothers. 'My mum isn't here. Dad is, though.'

Mrs Clifford smiled. 'Can I come in to speak to him?'

Elma wondered if she could say no, but then her dad called from the TV room. 'Bring the woman in, Elma, there's a love.'

Elma beckoned Mrs Clifford into the hall and closed the door behind her. Then she hesitated. The TV room was filthy, but the kitchen was totally impossible, as the baked beans that weren't dripping down Zac's t-shirt were spattered all over the table and the floor.

Reluctantly she opened the TV room door, and ushered Mrs Clifford towards her unshaven, grubby-looking father. Then she closed the door, and went back to begin tidying the kitchen.

Before long, Mrs Clifford appeared in the kitchen.

'May I sit down?' she asked.

Elma shrugged, so Mrs Clifford sat down on top of a small pile of beans that had slid from the table onto the chair.

She took out a notebook. 'You must be Elma, Dylan and Zac.'

Zac grinned at her. 'How did you know?' he asked. Elma glared at him, and he put his head down and looked at the floor.

Mrs Clifford spoke softly. 'It's my job to know that kind of thing. Now, why don't we all have a nice chat?'

Zac smiled again, until he saw his sister's angry face. Mrs Clifford cleared her throat. 'Who minds you after school?'

Dylan spoke quickly, sure he knew the right answer. 'Elma does. She's very good at minding us. She brings us home from school. She gets our tea, and helps us with our homework. She's great. She–'

Elma knew for sure that this was the wrong answer. She knew that kids weren't meant to be minding other kids. She put her hand on Dylan's arm to make him stop talking. 'Thanks, Dyl,' she said. 'I just help out a bit. But we all know that it's Dad who really minds us, don't we?'

Dylan looked at her for a moment. He knew she did all the work, and it wasn't fair to let their dad get all the credit. He jumped up. 'No, he doesn't. He doesn't do anything. He just lies on the couch and does a big fat nothing all day long.'

Mrs Clifford wrote something down in her notebook, and then she turned to Elma. 'It sounds like you're a very good girl. But what happens when you go out with your friends? Or when you do after-school activities? Who looks after the boys then?'

Out with her friends? What friends? Elma thought angrily. There was only Tara, and she was getting fed up of Elma always saying 'no' to stuff.

And what *after-school activities*? She hadn't done anything for years. For Elma, after-school activities were only a distant memory. Nowadays her only after-school activity was doing the washing-up.

But she couldn't tell the truth. The truth would get everyone into trouble. So she just smiled and said, 'I like being with the boys. We have such fun. And Dad's always here if we need him. Everything here is just fine. You really don't have to worry about us.'

Mrs Clifford didn't reply. She closed her notebook, and stood up. 'When would be a good time to speak to your mother?'

Zac blurted out, 'She works every day. She– '

Elma interrupted him. 'She'll be here tomorrow afternoon.'

'Tell her I'll be here at four thirty,' said Mrs Clifford, and then she headed for the front door. Zac and Dylan began to giggle when they saw the clump of baked beans sticking to the back of Mrs Clifford's coat. Elma hushed them. There was nothing at all funny about any of this.

Next afternoon, Mum cancelled her cleaning job and walked home from school with Elma and the boys. Evil Josh hissed at Elma as they passed by, 'Gravy Davey. Lumpy Gravy Davey.'

Mum was puzzled. 'Why is that nasty boy calling you that?'

Elma spoke quickly, before Zac or Dylan could tell the truth. 'Oh, don't mind him, Mum. It's just Josh. He's crazy.'

When they got home, everyone scurried around trying to clean up and make the house look a bit normal. Dad even helped by chaining Snowball up in the shed, and then turning the TV down to normal volume levels. One of the other dinner ladies had told Mum that a house always seemed nice and safe if there was a smell of bread baking. Of course Mum was in so much of a rush that she just shoved a sliced loaf into the oven, and turned the heat up high. As Elma suspected, it wasn't a good idea to leave the wrapping on the bread, and by the time Mrs Clifford arrived, instead of a cosy baked-bread smell, the house smelled badly of burning paper.

Mrs Clifford spent ages talking to Mum. For most of the time Elma had her ear pressed to the kitchen door, so she knew what was going on. Basically, Mrs Clifford said that Dad wasn't competent to mind the children, and Elma was too young, and that if things didn't change very quickly, there would have to be further investigations about the welfare of the children.

After Mrs Clifford left, Elma went to where her mum was sitting in the kitchen.

'Can we get a babysitter, Mum?' she asked. Already she could imagine a real cool teenager, who'd do great things with her. She could teach her about hairstyles, and make-up and music and stuff.

Mum didn't even wonder how Elma knew what was going on. She shook her head sadly. 'No, love. That wouldn't work. Babysitters are very expensive. And beside, Social Services are already on our case. I don't want to give them any excuse to find fault with us. There's only one thing for it.'

Elma whispered. 'What's that?'

'I'll have to give up my cleaning jobs. I'll have to spend the afternoons here with you.'

She gave a sudden tired smile. 'Let's look on the bright side. At least I'll be able to make your tea every evening.'

Elma tried to smile back. 'Sounds great, Mum.' Inside she was crying. Baked beans were a bit boring, but at least they weren't likely to poison you.

Her mum patted her hand. 'Don't worry, love. I've probably been asking you to do too much anyway. Maybe this is all for the best.'

Elma closed her eyes and tried to tell herself that things would be better from now on. She made a list of nice stuff in her head:

1. She'd be able to visit Tara's house after school
2. She could join some after-school clubs
3. She wouldn't have to do so much cooking and cleaning
4. She wouldn't have to mind the boys all the time.

But the nice list kept evaporating as the one big bad thing galloped around her brain – Mum was going to be home more, so there would be more time for her and Dad to fight.

Elma didn't have to wait long. The first big row

began as soon as the boys went to bed that night. As her parents screamed at each other, Elma took out Luke's last letter and read it. She was glad the stamp was upside down again.

She addressed her envelope, stuck the stamp upside down, and began to write. At first she wrote the usual lies, but as she signed the letter and folded it, there was a loud slam of a door, and then the TV began blaring out something about a hill-tribe in Thailand.

Elma began to cry. Life was just going to turn into a big long series of fights. Dad *had* to get his act together. He had to shake himself up and get a life again, before he ruined everyone else's. But how could Elma make that happen? She had no good ideas, and there was no one she could talk to. There was no one with whom she could share the awful truth.

Elma made a sudden decision. Luke Mitchell was a stranger. It wouldn't matter if she told him a small bit of the truth. And maybe he'd have an idea of how she could help her dad. She unfolded the letter, picked up her pen, and wrote a long PS.

Then, before she could change her mind, she folded the letter again, put it into its envelope, and sealed it.

Dear Luke,

Poor you, being mugged. I'm glad you got better quickly. It's kind of you to buy your mother a washing machine. The biggest thing I ever got my mum was a bottle of perfume that cost eight pounds. It lasted a whole year.

Jessica can walk really well now, and she knows lots of hard words. We think she might be a genius.

I hope you had a happy birthday. You didn't say if you got a new racehorse for Christmas. Maybe you got one for your birthday instead.

Bye,
Elma

PS Do you mind if I ask you something? Remember I told you my dad had an accident? Well he still isn't very well, and he can't go back to work yet. I think he's getting a bit fed up. He hasn't got any hobbies or anything. He just spends all day watching the National Geographic Channel on TV. Mum and I are trying to get him to go out more, but he won't listen to us. What would you do if you were me?

LUKE

Helen had some terrible disease. She was probably going to die.

There was no other way to explain what was going on. She was definitely sick – Luke had heard her throwing up in the bathroom loads of times in the last few weeks. And then last night, when he was lying in bed trying to sleep, he heard Mam coming home from work, and then Helen opening her bedroom door and going downstairs.

And for what seemed like a long time, he could hear their voices going back and forth in the kitchen. Helen sounded like she was crying, and Mam – Luke couldn't decide what Mam sounded like. He must have fallen asleep then, because he didn't remember them coming upstairs, but there was no sign of Helen at breakfast.

'Is Helen sick?' Luke asked his mother.

She nodded, looking paler than usual. 'She won't be going to school today.'

And when Luke came home that afternoon, Granny told him that Mam and Helen were gone to the doctor's, which meant that Helen had to be seriously ill. Mam didn't believe in going to the doctor unless you were really bad – she always said most things could be cured with a visit to the chemist, which cost nothing. The only time she'd taken Luke to the doctor's was when he got really bad sunburn years ago, and started throwing up all over the place.

Now he closed the Harry Potter book he'd bought with Granny's Christmas book token and looked out the window again. Almost time for tea, and still no sign of them. He remembered when Helen had stayed out all night, about three months ago now. He remembered wondering if she was dead, if her picture would be in the paper.

What if she died now? What if Mam came back alone from the doctor's and told them that Helen had been rushed into hospital, and she had only a few weeks, or even a few days, left to live? Would Anne be allowed in to say goodbye to her, when she was only seven?

Luke was glad he'd got Helen the HMV token for Christmas, even though she still hardly ever spoke to him. No wonder she was always so sad and cross looking, if she had some kind of terrible disease. That would make anyone sad and cross.

Helen and Mam came home at twenty-five to seven, just as Granny was putting two plates of food into the oven to keep warm. Helen looked as if she'd been crying again, and went straight upstairs.

Mam took off her coat and sat at the table. 'I've got something to tell you,' she said to Luke and Anne. Luke glanced at Granny, who was taking Mam's plate out of the oven. She didn't look curious – she must know already.

'Helen is … ' Mam paused, ran a hand through her hair. Anne and Luke waited. Luke felt suddenly afraid.

'Helen is … going to have a baby.' Mam looked from Anne to Luke. 'In June, she's having a baby in June.' She lifted her shoulders, let them drop again. 'That's it.'

Anne said, 'But where is she getting it from?'

A tiny smile passed over Mam's face. 'From heaven, where I got you.' Mam looked at Luke. 'What do you think?'

Luke hadn't a clue what to think. Helen was pregnant, not dying. She was going to have a baby. Her tummy was going to swell up like a watermelon, and she was going to have a baby, and be its mother.

And – the thought struck him like a shock – he was going to be its uncle. Uncle Luke. And Mam was going to be a granny, and Granny was going to be a great-granny.

Luke considered. It didn't seem so bad really. Another thought occurred to him. 'Will it live here, with us?' He tried to imagine a baby in the house, filling the place with nappies and bottles and crying in the middle of the night. A buggy in the hall. Teddies on the stairs.

Mam was frowning. 'None of that has been decided yet,' she told them. 'We'll have to sort out a lot of things.'

'You'll be its auntie,' Luke told Anne, and the uncertain expression left her face and she burst into a smile.

'Will I be able to feed it?' she asked Mam, and Mam shrugged.

'We'll see, lovie,' she said. 'It's a long way off.'

When he went upstairs later to do his homework, Luke paused outside Helen's door and listened. Nothing. He put up a hand and tapped lightly.

'Who is it?'

'Luke.' He waited for her to tell him to get lost, but after a second, Helen appeared at the door.

'Yeah?' She didn't look cross, just a bit tired.

'Mam told us,' Luke said. And then he wasn't sure what to say next.

Helen looked at him. 'So,' she said, 'what do you think?'

Luke risked a tiny smile. 'I think I'm going to be an uncle,' he said. He waited for the door to slam in his face.

Helen looked at him blankly for a few seconds, and then she gave a shaky smile back at him. 'Uncle Luke,' she said. 'Go and do your homework.' He'd almost forgotten what she looked like when she smiled.

In his room, Luke reread his penfriend's letter. And then he read the last bit twice more. It was a bit weird, the way both their fathers had something wrong with them. Her dad sounded very like Luke's, sitting around all day doing nothing much. So all her stories about going to Disneyland Paris and bowling and everything must have been made up, just like Luke had made up things. The thought didn't make him cross with her – more like a bit sorry for her. It was no fun having a dad that didn't want to do anything with you any more.

And now she was asking Luke's advice – like she thought he really might be able to help. What on earth should he say to her? He had enough problems with his own father, let alone anyone else's.

He put her letter aside while he did his homework, but all the time he was writing out his sums, or going over the dates of the Second World War battles, or practising the new tin whistle tune Mrs Hutchinson had given them to learn, Luke's mind kept tiptoeing back to Elma's letter, and the questions she'd asked him.

When his homework was finished, Luke went back downstairs and knocked softly on his father's door. After a few seconds he opened it and walked in and sat in his usual chair in the half-dark, breathing in the scent of his sleeping father.

What should he say to Elma? He had to say something, couldn't just ignore her questions when he wrote back. He sat by his father's bed, thinking hard.

After about fifteen minutes he got up, touched his father's warm cheek, and left the room. Then he poked his head around the sitting room door and told Granny he was going to bed.

'Right, lovie, see you in the morning.' She turned back to the TV.

Luke stood with his hand on the door. After a minute he said, 'Granny?'

'Yes, love?' His grandmother looked at him enquiringly.

'What do you think about this baby?' Luke asked.

Granny thought for a few seconds. Then she said, 'Well, it's not the way any of us would have wanted it, but we'll have to make the best of it now, won't we?'

Luke nodded. 'You'll be its great-granny.'

Granny smiled. 'So I will,' she said. 'Now there's a thought.'

In his room, Luke opened the box of notelets that Granny had given him for his birthday. They all had paintings of the sea on them. He picked a stormy one, with huge white-capped waves dashing against grey and black rocks.

He stuck his stamp on upside down, addressed the envelope and began his letter to Elma.

Dear Penfriend,

Here's a bit of news for you. My sister Helen is going to have a baby. It's not the way we would have wanted it, but we're going to make the best of it. The baby is coming in June, and I'll be its uncle. I've never been an uncle before, so I've got a lot to learn.

Still no sign of the gang who mugged me. The guards say they could have fled the country by now. If you see them in Manchester let me know, ha ha.

For my birthday I got a box of notelets from my granny, a new pair of jeans and trainers from my mam, a picture from Anne and a lottery scratchcard from Helen. I didn't win anything on the scratchcard. This is one of the notelets I'm writing on.

I'm sorry your dad is fed up. I've never seen the National Geographic Channel on TV – we don't have cable in our house, and I don't watch a lot of telly anyway. But we have a collection of National Geographic magazines in our class that our teacher brought in to help us with our geography projects, so I'm guessing that the TV channel has the same kind of stuff on it. If your dad watches it a lot, he must be a real expert on geography by now. Maybe he could get a job writing geography books for schools – or is there any quiz show on radio or TV that he could go on, or something? That's all I can think of for now.

It's funny your dad being like that – I don't mean funny, I mean strange, because something happened to my dad too, a few years ago. It's a long story, maybe I'll tell you sometime.

Anyway, that's all for now,
Luke

ELMA

The next few weeks were very, very bad. Mum and Dad spent most of the time fighting, and Elma and the boys spent most of their time in their bedroom pretending not to notice the screams and shouts and banging doors from downstairs.

Mrs Clifford called twice, and each time everyone pretended to be happy, just so she'd go away.

Twice Elma went to Tara's house after school. It was really fun to be in a house where people seemed to be happy, but when she was leaving the second time, Tara's mum stopped her in the hallway.

'It was lovely to see you, Elma,' she said. 'Maybe you'd like Tara to visit your house next time?'

'I don't think so,' Elma said, 'My house is kind of boring.'

Tara's mum just shook her head, and said nothing, but after that Tara kept on saying she'd love to visit Elma's house, and Elma couldn't think of any more lies or excuses, so now she mostly avoided Tara, and walked around the playground on her own.

One morning, Mrs Lawrence came into the classroom holding a big bundle of penfriend letters. She handed them out, saying, 'Don't open these until this afternoon; you are in year five now so I know I can trust you. Now, take out your maths books.'

But Mrs Lawrence was wrong to trust Elma, even though she was in year five. Elma just *had* to know what Luke Mitchell had written in his letter. Of course she didn't care about his stupid granny and her cakes, or about his imaginary dead horse or how many months old he was or any of that stuff. All she wanted to know was his answer to her question about her dad.

Maybe Luke Mitchell had come up with a super-fantastic idea to get Dad out of the house; if he hadn't, she just didn't know what she was going to do.

And so, while everyone else was puzzling over stupid maths problems, like how many buckets you'd need to carry a hundred and seven and a half litres of water, Elma spent some time puzzling over her problem family.

She tucked Luke's letter into her cardigan pocket, and asked to go to the toilet. Mrs Lawrence nodded, and Elma practically ran out of the room. She locked herself into a cubicle and ripped open the envelope. She didn't bother to admire the notelet with its picture of a stormy sea. She opened it, and skimmed through all the boring stuff. Then she got to the important bit. She read it, and then she read it once more. She couldn't help feeling disappointed.

Dad write geography books? Fat chance. Dad never even wrote as much as a letter. He couldn't write a geography book to save his life.

And a quiz? What good was a quiz? And what were the chances of there being a geography quiz conveniently running that her dad could just enter and win. As far as she knew, her dad had never entered a quiz in his life. So, even if there was a quiz, surely he'd just say no. Like he said no to everything else she suggested.

Elma crumpled up the notelet and crammed it into her pocket. She'd been right all along – Luke Mitchell was nothing but a stupid, boastful liar.

That afternoon was free activity time. It was her turn to use the computer, and she was allowed to pick someone to work with her. She went up to Tara.

'Do you want to do computer with me?'

Tara gave her a funny look. 'What do you want me for? I've noticed how you've been avoiding me, you know.'

Elma looked guilty. She was asking Tara because she had no one else to ask. So she smiled her best smile and said, 'Sorry, Tara. I've just been a bit worried about something, that's all.'

And Tara smiled back, and they both went to log on to the computer.

Tara wanted to go on to a site where you could design your own sports shoes, but Elma hesitated.

'Do you mind if I try something quick first?'

Tara shrugged, so taking that as permission, Elma opened a search engine, and quickly typed in two words: *Geography Quiz.* She made a face when the search result showed there were 240,000 pages about geography quizzes. Then she tried *Geography Quiz* and *UK*. This brought it down to 30,000 – still not much good.

Tara was starting to look impatient so Elma tried one more time: *Geography Quiz* and *UK* and *radio.* Then she closed her eyes and crossed her fingers and hit enter one more time. This time, there were only a few hundred hits, and the first one almost jumped off the screen and smacked her in the face. She quickly clicked on it and was directed into the BBC website. There, in the middle of a big red flashing circle, were the magic words: *The Great BBC Geography Quiz. Only six more days to enter.*

Elma quickly clicked on the words, and was directed to the competition page. Luckily, there was a phone number. She wrote it on the back of her hand, and then read the rest of the instructions: *Just telephone us before April 10th, and answer eight or more of the ten qualifying questions to be eligible for your regional final.*

Tara was puzzled. 'What's all this about?' she asked. 'Are you planning to enter that quiz? I didn't know you liked geography that much.'

Elma shook her head. 'It's not for me. I'm looking it up for my dad. He loves quizzes, and he really, really wants to enter this one.' This, of course, wasn't true, but Elma had made up her mind that her dad was going to enter this quiz whether he wanted to or not. She simply wasn't going to give him a choice in the matter.

Tara shrugged. 'Whatever. Now can we do something interesting?'

At lunchtime, Elma was so excited that she didn't even notice the huge pile of soggy carrots and lumpy gravy that her mum served her. And when school was over, she practically skipped all the way home.

And when Mum and Dad argued over what to have for tea, Elma didn't even listen.

Then, at about four o'clock, her opportunity arrived. Mum decided to go to the shops, and she took Zac and Dylan with her. As soon as they were gone, Elma took the portable phone into the kitchen, and dialled the competition number. A bored-sounding woman answered.

'BBC Geography Quiz. Name, please."

Elma hesitated. 'Er … em … Elma. Elma Davey.'

The woman suddenly seemed to pay attention. 'How old are you, Elma?'

'Eleven – well, nearly twelve.'

'I'm sorry. You need to be eighteen to enter the quiz. Thank you for calling.'

'No, wait,' Elma said before the woman could hang up. 'It's not me. It's my dad who wants to enter.'

'So why didn't *he* make the call?

Because he doesn't want to do anything except lie on the couch and watch TV, and I'm hoping that if I hand him the phone there's just a teensy weensy chance he won't argue, and he might answer a few geography questions without thinking too much about it.

She couldn't say that, though, so she thought quickly and said, 'Well, he *did* call. But while he was waiting for an answer, my baby sister started to cry, so he asked me to hold the phone. I think she's stopped crying now, I'll go and get him.'

She ran into the TV room, and bravely turned off the television.

Dad glared at her. 'What the–'

Elma pointed to the phone in her hand, and whispered, 'It's a quiz. A geography quiz. You only have to answer ten questions. And they'll be easy for you, 'cause you're so good at geography.'

Dad said something under his breath about 'stupid quizzes', but Elma smiled to herself as he reached for the phone.

He gave his name, and said yes and no a few times, and then Elma could see by the concentrated look on his face that he was being asked the first question. He wrinkled up his forehead as he thought. 'Papua, New Guinea,' he said.

Elma crossed her fingers, and tried to cross her toes, probably impossible for anyone, and certainly impossible for someone wearing too-small trainers.

Then something very strange happened. A smile, something she hadn't seen on her dad's face in a very long time, began to lurk at the corners of his mouth. Before she could say anything, he spoke into the phone again. And again. And again.

'Green.'

'Seven.'

'White with pink spots.'

'The Sumatran hare.'

'The Brazilian rainforest.'

'Once a year.'

With each answer, Dad's smile became broader and broader. Elma hardly dared to breathe. She'd lost count of how many questions he'd answered.

Then he answered three in a row, very quickly.

'Autumn.'

'The Zambezi.'

'The giant armadillo.'

And then Dad jumped up and actually punched the air. Next he made a shaky gesture with his hand that either meant he had completely lost his marbles, or else he wanted Elma to get a pen.

Elma raced into the kitchen, grabbed a pen and a scrap of paper, and ran back to the TV room. Dad took the pen and quickly wrote down a date, a time and an address. Then he clicked off the phone and dropped down heavily on to the couch, where he sat with a huge grin on his face. He didn't even reach for the remote. He spoke, half to himself, and half to Elma.

'Ten out of ten I got. She said that's very rare. She sounded like she was really impressed. And now I'm in the regional final. It's the BBC. Imagine me, Michael

Davey, on BBC radio. Whoever would have thought?'

Then he stopped and thought for a minute, and the smile vanished from his face. He put his head in his hands and groaned. 'How could I be so stupid? What was I thinking of? That can't have been a real quiz. It must have been some prankster. Why on earth would the BBC phone me?'

Elma jumped up, desperate to get her dad smiling again. 'Actually, Dad, they didn't phone you.'

Dad shook his head sadly. 'I knew it. A stupid wind-up. I just knew it. I–'

Elma rushed to correct him. 'No, Dad, it's not a wind-up. It's real. But they didn't phone you. *I* phoned *them*.'

Dad looked at her with a puzzled expression on her face. 'But why would you do that?'

She spoke in a rush. 'Because I saw it on the Internet. And there were only six days left. And I wanted you to enter. And I knew you'd say no. And I knew you'd win. And ... ' Her voice trailed off, and then she spoke softly. 'I just wanted you to do it, that's all.'

And Dad smiled at her, and rubbed her cheek, and for the first time in a very long time it looked like, maybe, just maybe, things were going to get better.

When Mum came home and heard the news, she

and Dad hugged, and that was such an unusual sight that Zac and Dylan got all giddy, and danced around, and Elma thought that if things went on like this it would be sooo embarrassing, but at least it would be an improvement, and so she joined in the dancing too, and all the Daveys were happy at the same time.

There were only a few rows that night, and they were small ones. And things weren't perfect over the next week or two, but they were a whole lot better than before.

A week later, when Mrs Lawrence said there was only one day left to send off the next penfriend letter, Elma remembered that she'd been so busy not being unhappy that she'd forgotten to thank Luke Mitchell. So that night she sat down and tried to decide what she should say. She thought of telling Luke the truth at last, but she couldn't really figure out a good way to do it.

How could she say – thanks for giving me such a great idea that might well change my life, and by the way, I spend most of my time thinking you are stupid? Oh, and by the way again, I've told you nothing but lies since September?

And so she began to write.

Dear Fantastic Super-clever Luke Mitchell,

That was such a good idea (the one about the quiz). Can you believe there was a quiz on the BBC, and I phoned and entered my dad without telling him, and he got ten out of ten in the qualifying round, and now he's going to be in the regional final? Maybe you can't believe it, because I can't really believe it either, and I was there. He was sooooo brilliant. We are all much happier already.

Jessica doesn't understand what's going on, but she's happy because Dad's happy. Mum made a special celebration dinner with all her best recipes. It was totally yummy and I had two helpings of everything and lots of extra gravy.

You're lucky you're going to be an uncle. I only have one uncle. He lives in Australia and he sends me money for my birthday and at Christmas. If you want to be a good uncle, maybe you should be like that. (Not living in Australia, of course, but giving the baby lots of money.) (But only when the baby is big enough, or it might choke.)

What happened to your dad? I suppose he's better now since he's able to take you climbing in the Pyrenees.

Goodbye and a big big big Thank You,
Elma

LUKE

'I'm going to be an uncle,' Luke told Jenny when he went to make his second payment on the washing machine.

Jenny looked up from the receipt she was writing out and beamed. 'Why that's wonderful news,' she said. 'You must all be delighted.'

'I'm going to be an uncle,' Luke told the man in the newsagents when he went to wash the two cars.

The man in the newsagents, whose name was Pat, gave Luke a slap on the back. 'Great,' he said. 'Well done.' Which sounded a bit strange to Luke, as he hadn't done anything.

'I'm going to be an uncle,' Luke told Mrs Hutchinson at break.

Mrs Hutchinson's eyes widened. 'Are you now?' she said. 'Helen, is it?' Mrs Hutchinson had taught Helen in sixth class too.

Luke nodded. 'She's going to have a baby in June.'

'I see,' said Mrs Hutchinson. She didn't look happy, like Jenny or Pat the newsagent.

'I'm going to be an uncle,' Luke told his uncle Jack, when Jack came to collect him as usual on Saturday morning.

Jack nodded. 'Your mam rang us,' he said. 'That's a bit of a surprise, isn't it?'

'I thought Helen was sick,' Luke told Jack. 'I thought she was going to die.'

Jack smiled. 'You're a funny one,' he said. 'Your mam told us about the washing machine too – that was a nice thing you did.'

Luke wondered if he could tell Jack about the boy who had taken his money. He wondered if he could tell him about seeing the boy in town the other day. Luke wasn't absolutely certain it was the same boy, but he was wearing a grey hoodie and a black scarf, and he looked about the right height. He was standing on the path with two other boys, and they were all smoking, holding their cigarettes cupped in their hands to keep the wind off them.

But Luke said nothing to Jack. There was no point

in saying anything now. The money was probably all spent anyway, on cigarettes, or beer or something.

'Helen's having a baby,' he said to his father. 'In June.'

His father looked back at him. 'Helen,' he said.

'She's having a baby,' Luke said again. 'You're going to be a granddad.'

And then something amazing, and a little frightening, happened. His father's face seemed to soften around the edges, and a tear trickled from the corner of one eye and rolled down his cheek. 'Granddad,' he repeated softly. He lifted his arm and rubbed the sleeve of his jumper across his face.

Luke watched two more tears trickling slowly down his father's face. 'It's OK,' he said, feeling a bit scared. He'd never seen his father cry, ever. 'It's just a baby, don't be sad.' He took his father's hand and held it between his own two. 'It's OK, Dad, really.'

His father wiped his face with his jumper sleeve again. Then he smiled shakily at Luke. 'Baby,' he whispered.

And Luke understood that he wasn't crying because he was sad.

Granny was knitting tiny clothes. Every night when she settled in front of the telly she clicked her needles and grew a little yellow jumper, or a pair of teeny white socks, or a pale green hat that just about covered Luke's fist.

Anne was making mobiles for the baby. She drew stars and flowers and smiley faces, and cut them out. Then she poked a hole in them with a needle and hung them with thread from coat hangers.

On her day off, Mam took down all the posters in Helen's bedroom and painted over the shabby wallpaper. When Helen came home from school she walked into a wonderful buttery yellow room, full of light. She flew downstairs and hugged Mam, nearly knocking over the pan full of sausages.

Helen and Mam were friends again. Luke wasn't sure how it had happened, or when, but there were no more rows, or slamming doors, or phone calls from the pub to check if Helen was at home. And the sad, worried look began to fade slowly from Mam's face. One morning Luke heard her humming along to the radio in the kitchen.

And Helen was talking to everyone again, not just Mam. Every day she was becoming more and more like the Helen Luke remembered. She even helped him revise for his spelling test last week.

And in the past ten days, Anne hadn't wet the bed once.

The car washing was going well. Luke had five

regular customers now, as well as Pat the newsagent and his wife. And he still went out to Jack's farm every Saturday. Even with the fifty euro a month he was paying for the washing machine, he was still managing to save a fair bit.

He was thinking about a cot, when he had enough. He might just make it by June.

His penfriend's last letter had taken him by surprise. He'd forgotten about suggesting some kind of quiz for her father, hadn't really thought any more about it after he'd sent off the letter. Imagine that Elma had actually thought his idea was good, and entered her father in a quiz, and now he was through to some finals.

He liked being called Fantastic Super-clever Luke Mitchell. It made him feel like some kind of hero, even if he hadn't really done anything to deserve it. But it was good that his idea had helped Elma's dad.

Pity he'd made up all that stuff about his own dad, though. Climbing in the Pyrenees indeed. Luckily, Elma seemed to have forgotten all that stuff about his dad being an astronaut. But now she wanted to know what happened him – served Luke right for saying anything about that.

Should he come clean now, and tell her the whole truth? Would she be shocked at all the stories he'd made up? Maybe she'd stop writing to him altogether. Mrs Hutchinson said she hoped the class would keep in contact with their penfriends even after they'd left primary school. She said it could be the start of a lifelong friendship. A couple of the girls in the class said they were planning to visit Manchester in the summer and meet up with their penfriends.

Luke stuck on his upside-down stamp and wrote Elma's name and school address on the envelope. Then he picked out a sunny seaside notelet – blue skies, yellow sand, people splashing in the foamy water – and began his letter.

Dear Penfriend,

I'm glad your dad is feeling better. Let me know how he gets on in the quiz.

I'd like to visit Australia. Maybe when I'm an uncle I'll go there, ha ha. I have an uncle called Jack who lives a few miles from us, and he has a farm where I help out on Saturdays.

My granny is knitting teeny clothes for the baby. They look like they're for a doll. I don't think I was ever that small.

I know you asked me about my dad, but I don't want to talk about what happened to him, except to say that when it happened, it changed everything, and for a long time our house was not a good place to live in. But I think things are getting a bit better now. I hope so anyway.

Now I must revise for tomorrow's history test.
Luke

PS I hope this doesn't make you cross, but I made that up about climbing in the Pyrenees. I don't know why I did it really.

ELMA

Everyone was a bit tense on the days leading up to the regional final. There were lots of fights, but then that was nothing new for the Davey family. On the day of the competition, however, everyone was in a great mood. It was a Saturday, so the whole family was able to go to cheer Dad along. Zac even wanted to bring Snowball, managing to forget in all the excitement that he was actually terrified of the huge Alsatian. Luckily, Mum said no, she didn't think they'd be able to get him past the security guards at the BBC.

Dad spent ages getting ready. He'd had his hair cut the day before, and now he shaved off his straggly beard and moustache. Elma met him on the stairs, and almost jumped back in fright. All of a sudden it was as if the ghost of the dad she used to know had come crawling back from wherever it had been hiding for the last few years.

When everyone else was ready to go, Dad appeared in the hall. He was wearing a freshly ironed, crispy white shirt, and new jeans. Dylan gasped. 'Dad, you look great,' he said. 'But it's radio, remember. No one will see you.'

Dad patted his shoulder. 'Appearances are important, kiddo, never forget that.'

Elma giggled. Dad seemed to have forgotten about that for the past three years, while he was lounging around the house in his shabby old tracksuit. She didn't say anything, though. There was no way she was going to mess up this special day.

Mum drove them all to the BBC studios. Elma couldn't remember when the whole family had been in the car together before. When they got there, everyone got special security passes, and went to wait in a big green room. While they were waiting, Elma saw a famous TV chef walking past. She wondered if she should grab him and persuade him to give her mum a few cookery lessons. But while she was wondering, he vanished into a room and the moment had passed.

Four other contestants arrived. They hadn't brought their families with them, and Elma wondered if Dad felt a bit stupid now. No one said very much. Then Zac nudged Dylan and pointed to a skinny man in the corner, and said in a much-too-loud whisper, 'He doesn't look very clever. Dad will easily beat him.'

Everyone laughed nervously, and then sat in uneasy silence until the contestants were called. Dad looked very scared as he followed the others out of the room. Elma gave him a thumbs-up sign, and a smile she didn't feel like. For the first time, she began to wonder if her plan was such a good one. What if Dad made a complete fool of himself? What would happen then? And she'd boasted about this at school, so everyone would be listening. How would she face school on Monday if Dad came last? Evil Josh would have one more thing to tease her about, and surely Tara would finally give up on her as a total loser.

The quiz was going to be broadcast live. There was a speaker in the corner of the room, so the family could listen. There was lots of music, and boring talk, and then the presenter said, 'And now it's time for the Manchester regional final of this year's Great Geography Quiz.'

Everyone sat up straight and giggled excitedly as

the contestants introduced themselves.

'That's Dad,' said Zac when he heard his father's voice, like no one else had noticed.

Next the presenter explained the rules. It was all buzzer questions. If you buzzed and got the answer right, you got two points, but if you got it wrong, two points would be deducted from your score. There was a huge drum-roll, and then the quiz began.

Mum grabbed Elma's hand and squeezed it tight. Zac and Dylan sat with tense, serious faces. The first round was over very quickly, and Dad hadn't buzzed once. Zac started to cry. 'Is it over? Dad didn't say anything.'

Elma spoke as brightly as she could. 'It's OK, Zaccy. Dad's just warming up. There's four more rounds.'

Round two started, and the family waited in vain to hear Dad's voice. Finally, halfway through the round, he buzzed for the question, 'In which country is Lake Volta?'

His voice was hoarse, and he sounded like he was miles away, even though Elma knew he was only just along the corridor. 'It's em, er … it's … I mean … it's … is it in Zambia?'

There was the dull thud of a gong, indicating a wrong answer. Elma looked at her mother, and noticed tears in her eyes. She wished she could run into the studio and shake her dad. It just wasn't fair. He knew more about geography than any of the others, she was sure of it. All he had to do was get his act together and start answering some questions.

Round two came to an end and the presenter called out the scores. There was a tie for first place with eighteen points, and Dad was bringing up the rear with a total of minus two points.

Elma jumped up and stamped her feet a few times, but it didn't make her feel any better. Dylan wanted to go home, but Elma knew they had to stay until the bitter end. Then they could all go home and be unhappy again.

Round three started, and Elma could hardly bear to listen. Then, on the fourth question she heard Dad's voice again. This time he got the answer right, bringing his score up to a grand total of zero. Then a minute later, he buzzed again, and got another two points. This was quickly followed by two more correct answers. Zac started to jump up and down. 'Is he winning?' he asked. 'Is he winning?'

Mum smiled at him. 'Not yet, love, but he's doing better.'

Dylan tapped Elma's arm. 'Is Dad going to win?'

Elma shrugged. All she knew was, if she wasn't

going to be the laugh of the school on Monday, Dad needed to answer a few more questions.

At the end of round three, there was still a draw for first place, and Dad was still last, but at least he was no longer quite as far behind.

Round four started well. Dad got the first four questions right. Zac and Dylan jumped around the room, and knocked over a huge plant. Leaves and soil went everywhere, but Mum wasn't even cross. She was staring at the radio speakers, like they held all the secrets of the universe. Then it seemed like Dad could do no wrong. He buzzed and buzzed, and only made one mistake. Round four ended, and now there was one leader, with Dad only six points behind her. Mum grinned at Elma. 'Six points,' she said. 'That's nothing. It's only three questions.'

Elma couldn't reply. She felt sick, and her hand hurt from her mum's tight grip.

Round five was very dramatic. It was almost as if the other contestants had given up, and mostly it was just Dad and a woman who were answering. Elma struggled to keep score on her fingers, wishing the quiz could have been on TV so at least the score would be on a screen.

After what felt like a hundred years, a bell rang, signaling the end of the show. The presenter called out the results, starting with fifth place. Then he called out fourth and third, but there was no mention of Dad. Elma could hardly breathe. Dad was first or second. Second would be good, but not good enough to get him to the national finals. The presenter took a deep breath. 'And in a very noble second place, we have .... Suzanne Wall.'

Now Mum and Elma joined in Zac and Dylan's crazy dance. Dad had won! Elma could hardly believe it. It seemed like all her wishes had just come true.

Shortly afterwards, Dad came back to the waiting room. He was grinning so much, Elma thought his face was going to burst. Everyone ran and hugged him tight until he begged for mercy. 'Back off, guys,' he said. "I need to be in good shape – for THE NATIONAL FINALS!!'

Then everyone was so happy they hugged him some more.

Finally Mum pulled away. 'Let's go home, and I'll cook a big celebration dinner,' she said. 'I'll do roast chicken, and roast potatoes, and carrots, and lots of gravy of course, and then–'

Elma's heart sank, but then her Dad interrupted. 'Thanks, love,' he said. 'That sounds lovely, but you could do with a rest. How about we all go out for a pizza?'

And then there was so much cheering and shouting that a security guard came to see what was going on.

Elma smiled when she read Luke's next letter. She couldn't really be cross about Luke lying about the climbing trip to the Pyrenees; not when most of what she wrote to him was still lies. This would be a good opportunity to tell Luke that she hadn't exactly been truthful herself, but she couldn't find the right words.

Dear Luke,

You are not going to believe this. <u>My Dad won the regional final of the Geography Quiz.</u> He was sooooo fantastic. He was on the radio, and everyone heard him. We were all very proud. Soon he's going to be in the UK final in London. The whole family is going there with him on the train. (But not Snowball, of course. She doesn't like travelling.) I can't wait. I just know Dad's going to win. He's going to be famous. And so am I because he's my dad. I always wanted to be famous.

Now maybe Mum won't bother writing the book about gravy and carrots. To be honest, I don't think it would ever have been a big success.

I'm sorry your dad never took you climbing in the Pyrenees. And I'm sorry about the bad thing (whatever it was) that happened to him. Is he any good at quizzes? – because that certainly worked for my dad.

Must go now and plan what to wear in London,
Elma

PS We've been writing to each other since forever. Why do you still call me Dear Penfriend instead of Dear Elma? Is it because you don't like my name? Don't blame me, because I didn't choose it. If I could have picked I would have called myself Saffron.

LUKE

Helen brought her boyfriend home for tea, so he could meet the family.

His name was Sean. He had short, light brown hair and pale blue eyes and a thin face scattered with little red spots. He brought a small box of chocolates for Mam when he came to tea, and an apple tart that his mother had made. He shook hands with their father and called him sir, and he didn't seem to notice that their father wasn't really interested in talking.

He blushed if anyone spoke to him, even Anne. He cut into his fried egg with the side of his fork, instead of using his knife, and he ate every bit of his rasher, even the skin. But he had a nice smile, and when he looked at Helen, his face went soppy.

He worked in the garage across the road from Helen's school, and he lived at home with his parents and older brother. He was almost eighteen, and he was training to be a mechanic. When Luke mentioned his car washing jobs, Sean said he could probably get Luke a few more customers.

Nobody at all mentioned the baby, not even Anne.

Granny made custard to go with the apple tart, and they all had a slice. Mam told Sean that he must get the recipe for her, and he blushed and smiled, and would have knocked over his water glass if Anne hadn't caught it just in time.

A whole month had gone by without Anne wetting the bed. Granny took her shopping one day for new socks, and they came home with three pairs of socks, a red dress and shiny red shoes. Mam laughed and said Granny would be broke from them.

The Saturday after Sean came to tea, Luke asked his uncle Jack if he had a camera.

'I have, a digital one,' Jack told him. 'Got it for Christmas.'

'Will you take my photo with Chestnut?' Luke asked him. 'I want to send it to a friend.' So Jack got his camera and took a few photos of Luke sitting on Chestnut's enormous back, and then he printed off the best one and gave it to Luke.

'Look,' Luke told his father. 'Here's me on Uncle Jack's horse.'

His father looked down at the photo. He touched Luke's face gently in the photo. 'Luke,' he said. 'Son and heir.'

He had mostly good days now, hardly ever sat facing the wall. Helen began reading bits of the paper to him when she came home from school, and Anne drew him pictures of cats and ballerinas and stuck them on the wall behind his bed.

And Mam was talking to him again. Luke heard her, in the bathroom when she was shaving him, or as she was helping him down the hall to the kitchen for tea. Luke heard her telling Dad how sweet Sean was, and how she was sure he'd stand by Helen, and how it looked like Anne was over the bed-wetting at last.

Dad didn't answer her much, but Mam kept on talking to him. And on her evenings off from work, she'd sit beside Dad's bed as he fell asleep, still talking softly. It was like she was telling him all the things that she'd saved up for the past three years.

On the day that Sean came to tea for the second time, Mam announced that she'd been promoted to branch manager in the travel agency, and now she could afford to give up doing the overtime in the evenings. The next day Granny baked a coffee cake and Helen wrote *Congratulations Mam* in purple icing when she came home from school, and Luke bought a bottle of sparkling grape juice, and they all drank a toast to Mam's promotion.

That night, Luke sat down to write to his penfriend. He wrote her address and stuck on his upside-down stamp, and then he folded up the photo of him and Chestnut and slid it into the envelope.

It was time to tell the truth. He sucked the end of his biro for a few minutes, and then he started his letter. And as he wrote, he felt something changing inside him, some heaviness falling away and leaving him with a feeling he couldn't name ...

... and as he got to the end of the letter, he decided it just might be happiness.

Dear Saffron,

I called you penfriend because I thought if I didn't use your real name, then I wouldn't be writing a real letter to a real person. I thought that it wouldn't matter what I wrote, that I could make up the craziest stories, and it wouldn't make one tiny bit of difference. It wouldn't be like telling fibs, or lies, because it was all imaginary. You were just part of my homework, that was all – nothing to do with real life. And if I called you penfriend, it made it easier to go on believing that.

Does any of that make sense? I hope so, because for the first time I'm writing the truth, the whole truth and nothing but the truth. This is the real story of Luke Mitchell, whether you want it or not.

I already told you that I made up the bit about climbing the Pyrenees with my dad. The truth is, for the past three and a half years, my dad hasn't been able to climb the stairs in our house. He sleeps in what used to be our dining room, and he has to use a walking frame, like old people use, to help him get around the downstairs.

He never goes out, except when my mam takes him for check-ups to the hospital, or when my uncle Jack, his brother, brings him out to the farm for a visit. He can't cut up food, or shave himself or even do a jigsaw properly.

The reason why my dad is like this is that he drove through a red traffic light and crashed into a jeep, and damaged his brain. I was in the car with him, but the only bad thing that happened to me was that I swallowed my two front teeth. (I have false ones now, that look just like the real thing.)

My mam was mad with my dad for a long time afterwards, because he drank two glasses of wine before he drove, and because I wasn't wearing my seat belt. (She was always very strict about wearing seat belts.) She didn't talk to my dad when he came home from hospital, even though she had to shave him and help him eat and lots of stuff like that.

Our house felt terrible, with Dad being the way he was, and Mam being mad at him. My sister Anne started wetting the bed, even though she was four at the time. My sister Helen (who isn't a model, just a schoolgirl) started staying out late and not telling us where she was going, and that caused a lot of rows with my mam.

Our granny moved in with us after Dad's accident, to help out, but she was often stuck in the middle of some row, and I was always afraid she'd go back to her own house, but she never did.

We don't live in a big fancy house. We live in a cul de sac, in a normal semi-detached house with four bedrooms, and we don't own any horses. The picture I'm sending you is of me on Uncle Jack's horse, Chestnut, which is the only horse I know. Chestnut never won a race in his life – he's a big farm horse who'd probably run the wrong way. But I ride him around Uncle Jack's field every Saturday, and I feed him apples.

You can see from the photo that I don't look a bit like I described myself. And in case you can't see clearly, I haven't anything pierced, or any tattoos either – I'm pretty sure Mam would kill me if I ever did anything like that.

The good news is that things have got a bit better lately. Everyone seems kind of happier. I'm not sure why, but I think in a funny sort of way, it has something to do with Helen having a baby, even though she's not married and only sixteen. But since she told us the news, she and Mam have stopped having rows, and Mam has started talking to Dad again. And Anne has stopped wetting the bed all the time.

My dad will never get better, and that makes me a bit sad, because I miss him a lot, all the time. You can't talk properly to him any more, because he doesn't really understand a lot of what you say. But most of the time now he seems quite happy, and that cheers me up too.

So now you know all my terrible secrets. I hope you're not too shocked, and I hope we can keep in touch. It's nice to have someone to talk to. Sorry this letter is so long.

Your penfriend,

Luke

PS I think the name Elma is OK. If I could pick a name for myself I'd go for Sam. I think it's nice and friendly.

ELMA

The next few weeks went by slowly. Mum seemed to be getting used to being at home in the afternoons, and wasn't so jumpy. Sometimes she sat down and read a magazine, or phoned a friend for a chat. Sometimes she even looked happy.

Dad still watched TV a lot, but now it was called *'research for the UK finals'*, and it didn't seem like such a waste of time. Also, he got dressed properly every day now, and most days he took Snowball for a walk, or took the boys to the park to play football. One day he went to the supermarket with Elma, and they bumped into Tara. Next day Tara said that Elma's dad seemed 'really nice,' and Elma floated around on a little puffy cloud of happiness all day long.

Then, just when Elma thought she was going to die from eating her mum's cooking, there was some really, really great news. The school got a grant to pay for a cookery course for one of the dinner ladies. Mum was picked (Elma could guess why), so there was real hope that in a few months they might even be eating food that tasted like food. And maybe, just maybe, soon she could invite Tara home without feeling she was risking her friend's life.

The day of the geography quiz final was wet and windy. Everyone got soaked on the way to the railway station, and shivered most of the way to London. Dad did his best to cheer them all up, but Elma couldn't help feeling that the day had started out badly, and was sure to continue in the same way.

The train ran late, and they got to the BBC just on time. Dad was whisked away, and Mum, Elma and the boys were led into a small room. There was a table with tea, coffee, and heaps of yummy-looking cakes. Mum drank litres of black coffee, and the boys ate most of the cakes, but Elma couldn't touch anything. She was so nervous she felt like she was going to throw up. She was so proud about Dad winning the regional final that she'd boasted to the whole school about it. So now everyone was going to be listening. If Dad did badly, she would never, ever hear the end of it.

Once again, there was a radio in the waiting room, and after ages, the quiz began. It was just like the regional final, with five contestants, and five rounds of buzzer questions.

The questions were very fast and it was hard to tell who was winning, but at the end of the first round, the scores were almost level, with Dad in joint second place.

At the end of round two, Dad was in second place on his own. Zac and Dylan did a little victory dance, scattering cake crumbs all over the carpet.

After round three, Dad had slipped into third place. Elma felt like crying.

Was Dad going to fall to pieces?

If he did, what would happen to them all?

There was a short break, and soft classical music began to play. Even Zac and Dylan were quiet, sitting pale-faced on a huge red leather sofa. Mum had her hands over her mouth, and her eyes looked tired and scared.

All of a sudden, Elma felt like walking away from the room, away from the BBC, away from her family. The whole quiz thing had been an impossible dream. How could she have thought that her dad could win a national quiz? She'd learned at school that there were almost sixty million people in the UK. How could Elma have thought that her dad could be better at geography than the other fifty-nine million and however many hundreds of thousands were left?

Just then, the music stopped, and round four began. Elma held her breath. Dad seemed to be doing OK. He was buzzing quite often, and never getting any questions wrong. At the end of the round, he was back in second place.

As the fifth and final round began, Elma laced her fingers together, and squeezed tightly until her fingertips began to turn white. She glanced at her mum, who seemed to be praying. The round seemed to be progressing in s-l-o-w m—o—t—i—o—n. It was almost as if the world had suddenly decided to turn at a more leisurely pace, just because Elma's dad was in the last round of the BBC geography quiz.

Elma stopped listening to the questions. There was a strange kind of buzzing in her ears, as if her brain had decided she couldn't listen any more. Soon Mum grabbed her arm. 'It's over,' she whispered. 'That was the last question.'

Elma felt like she was waking from a long sleep. 'And???'

Mum shook her head. 'I don't know. I lost count of the questions.'

The quiz presenter's voice interrupted. 'Well, that was a very interesting round, and at the end this is how things stand ... '

There was along silence. Elma felt like screaming. She wished she could run into the studio, find the presenter and shake him to make him call out the results quickly.

Finally the presenter continued, 'In fifth place ... Laura Wilson.' There was the sound of clapping from the other contestants. Elma wondered if Dad was clapping with the others. She wondered how he felt. Did he know who had won?

Was he glad he hadn't come last?

Was he glad he was here?

Or did he wish he was at home, lying on the couch, listening to Snowball snarling in the yard?

The presenter interrupted her thoughts. 'In fourth place ... James Dowling.' There was more polite clapping. Elma supposed that James Dowling wasn't clapping. Was he very upset because he'd come second last? Was he picking up his coat and getting ready to leave?

'In third place ... Amrita Sharma.'

Elma breathed again. Dad was first or second. She told herself either would be good, but in her heart she was fairly sure that second place wasn't good enough at all. First place would take the winner to Paris, for a big European competition. The person who came second would go back home with nothing but their tattered dreams and a souvenir mug.

This time the silence was so long that Elma began to wonder if the presenter had packed up his microphone and gone home. At last he spoke again. 'And now we have an interesting situation. It's a dead heat between Michael Davey and June Worth.'

Zac and Dylan began to jump up and down, screaming loudly. After a moment Dylan stopped. 'What does that mean, Mum? Does it mean Dad won? Is he the champion? Is he going to Paris?'

Mum put her arm around him. 'Shh, love. Listen and we'll know.'

The presenter spoke again. 'I'd like to congratulate all five contestants on an excellent competition. I have to say that the standard has been particularly high this year. Over the past few months ... '

Elma stamped her foot impatiently. 'Get on with it,' she muttered. 'Tell us what happens next.'

Finally the presenter got to the point. 'As we have two contestants with equal scores, we go to a sudden death.'

Zac went pale. 'That doesn't sound very nice.'

Elma had to laugh, but stopped quickly as the

presenter continued. 'I'll ask one question, and the first to buzz gets to answer. If he or she gets it wrong, I pass to the other contestant. Now, Michael, June, are you both ready?'

June's 'yes' was loud and clear. Dad's sounded like Snowball when he was having nightmares.

'And the deciding question is: In which country is the volcano Popocatepetl?'

There was another long silence. Elma jumped when the silence was broken by the shrill sound of a buzzer. The presenter spoke. 'And that was June. Your answer please.'

Elma began to chant in her head: *Get it wrong, get it wrong, please get it wrong.*

But June didn't get it wrong. She spoke loudly and clearly. 'Popocatepetl is in Mexico.'

'And we have a winner! Well done, June. You are this year's National Geography quiz winner. Well done to Michael Davey, a valiant contestant, in second place.'

There was more clapping. Elma could hear June Worth's gasps of disbelief. She wondered if all the other contestants hated her for winning the prize they so desperately wanted for themselves? Did Dad hate her? Elma certainly did. She hated June Worth even more than she hated Evil Josh. She hated June

Worth (whom she'd never even met) more than she had ever hated anyone in her entire life. June Worth had ruined everything.

Much later, Dad came back to the waiting area. He was smiling, but he looked like he really wanted to cry. Everyone hugged him, and tried to laugh when Zac said, 'I thought you were the best, Dad.'

The journey back to Manchester was a sad, quiet affair. Every now and then Dad broke the silence by saying, 'I knew it. I knew the answer.'

No one argued with him, but secretly Elma wondered if he was just pretending. Then, just as the train drew into the station, Dad spoke again. 'I knew it was in Mexico. I saw a programme about it last year. The name Popocatepetl means 'smoking mountain'. It was named by the Aztecs. It's near the city of Puebla. It's–'

Elma interrupted him. 'If you knew all that, why didn't you buzz?'

Dad sighed. 'I don't know, love. I knew the answer, and thought, now I just press the button, and then I looked at my finger, and I hesitated, and before I could move, the other woman buzzed, and it was all over.'

Elma didn't know what to say. Dad was right – it was all over.

There was no celebration dinner that night. Mum

just served up the usual mush.

In the morning, Dad wasn't up when everyone else left for school. Elma felt sure that it was back to the same old routine. Dad in front of the TV, avoiding his family, avoiding life.

School was OK. Evil Josh tried to tease Elma about her dad being a loser, but no one listened. One of the other boys pushed him away. Everyone crowded around Elma, and asked about her dad, and seemed to think that second place in the UK was a good result. And second place *was* a good result; it just wasn't quite good enough. If Dad could have got through to the European competition, the dream could have lived for just a bit longer. And without the dream, life would slip back to the way it used to be.

When she arrived home after school with Mum and the boys, Elma expected to see Dad lying on the couch, watching TV. The house was quiet, though, and it was unusually clean and tidy. Dad was sitting at the kitchen table with a bundle of books. There was a huge grin on his face.

Elma was afraid to ask what he was so happy about.

Luckily, Zac wasn't as cautious as Elma. 'What's going on, Dad?' he asked.

Dad grinned. 'What do you mean?'

Zac thought for a minute, then he rubbed his dad's chin. 'You've shaved. And the house is clean, and–'

Dylan continued. '–and the TV isn't on.'

Dad grinned again. 'No time for TV. I'm too busy now.'

Mum sat down and looked at Dad in disbelief. 'Too busy doing what?'

Dad grinned again. This was getting annoying. Elma felt like punching him, but hit the table instead. 'Just tell us, Dad. What's happened.'

'I'm going back to work.'

Now everyone else grinned, and blurted out their questions. 'Where?' 'How?' 'Why?' 'When?' 'Doing what?'

So Dad sat them down and explained that he'd gone to the job centre that morning. There he spoke to a job counselor, and he'd done an interview, and he was going to do a trial placement in the Animal Welfare centre. If it worked out, he could do a training course to be a vet's assistant. The placement started tomorrow, so would everyone please stop asking questions because he needed some peace and quiet to read up all the books he'd brought home.

After all the excitement had died down, Elma went to sit by her mum. 'Can I invite Tara over after school tomorrow?'

Mum smiled at her. 'Of course you can. Now, run upstairs and do your homework. I'll call you when dinner is ready. It's roast chicken.'

And Elma was so happy, even the thought of dinner couldn't spoil it.

In her bedroom, she pulled out the letter she'd got from Luke that morning. First she took out the photograph. He looked nice – kind of normal. He looked happy, too, sitting there on that huge old farmhorse. But hadn't he said before that he had black hair with blue tips? All along she'd been picturing someone else. She'd been writing lies to someone who didn't look a bit like this nice Irish boy.

She opened the letter and read through it one more time. All of a sudden, she felt guilty because her problems had all sorted themselves out. How pathetic she had been – upset because Dad had been injured by a toilet. And anyway, Dad was better now, not like Luke's dad, who was never going to recover. Poor Luke. No wonder he told as many lies as she had. Maybe telling the truth is only easy when you are happy.

She ran downstairs. 'Dad,' she said.

Dad looked up from his reading.

'Yes, love. What is it?'

'You know that mug you won, the BBC one?'

Dad nodded. 'What about it?'

'How badly do you want to keep it?'

Dad shrugged. 'I don't know. It's nice, but it's only a mug, I suppose. Why?'

Elma sat down beside him. 'Well, there's this boy, Luke. He's my penfriend. He's the one who gave me the idea about the geography quiz. And I'd like to send him something. So can I send him the mug?'

Dad smiled at her. 'Yes, I suppose you can. I'll get you some bubble-wrap later, so you can post it safely.'

Elma went to the shelf and took down the mug. As she left the kitchen, Dad called her back.

'That's very kind of you, Elma,' he said. 'This Luke is lucky to have a nice penfriend like you.'

Elma ran upstairs and tried not to think how not nice she had been to Luke in the beginning.

She took out her pen and paper and started to write.

Dear Sam,

I am so so so so sorry for your dad. It must be awful for you. My dad was bad, but he wasn't as bad as all that. And he's better already. Your suggestion about the quiz is what changed him. It kind of woke him up, if you know what you mean. You see, his back injury was better, but his mind seemed to have gone to sleep. He didn't win the geography quiz final, by the way. He came second. It doesn't matter, though. He's going back to work tomorrow, and we are all very happy about that.

I hope you like the mug I'm sending you. It's the one Dad got for being in the finals. I think you deserve it, because you gave me the idea of the quiz to start with. You can show it to your dad.

Tara says I should be cross with you for telling me so many lies. (But that's only because she doesn't know how many lies I've told you.) I probably can't remember them all, but these are the ones I can remember:

1. Dad didn't get hurt saving a little girl. He was unloading a lorry, and a toilet fell on him and injured his back. I think you can guess why I didn't tell the truth about that.

2. I don't have a little sister called Jessica. I just wish I did. I do have two little brothers, though. They're called Zac and Dylan. And they're quite nice (for boys).

3. Snowball isn't a cute furry cat. He's a huge, ugly, mean-tempered Alsatian with bad breath and wiry hair.

4. My mum is probably the worst cook in the world, and she

doesn't work in a fancy restaurant – she's a dinner lady at my school.

So that's it. They're the biggest lies. I think I made up stuff because I didn't like the truth.

It's nearly summer holidays here, and next year I'm going to a new school. I'd like to promise to write to you, but soon it won't be my homework any more, and I'm a bit lazy, so please try to understand if I don't write.

If I do write to you, I'm going to put my stamp on upside down. I'm always going to do that from now on. So even in fifty years time, if you get a letter with an upside-down stamp, you'll know it's from me.

I hope Helen has a lovely baby. (If it's a girl she might have long blonde hair and you could call her Jessica.)

I hope you have a nice life.
Your ~~best~~friend
Saffron (Elma)